The Waiter and Mrs. Davis

By

Keith P. Mulrooney

Started: 2/22/2022

Completed: 1/19/2025

The Waiter and Mrs. Davis
By: Keith P. Mulrooney

Table of Contents

The Waiter and Mrs. Davis
By: Keith P. Mulrooney

The Del-Ray is a name synonymous with luxury and refinement, its reputation built on lavish design elements and timeless elegance in Montclair County. Step inside, and you are enveloped by the warm glow of fumed oak paneling, the intricate craftsmanship of a coffered oak-beamed ceiling, and the shimmer of silver chandeliers. The richly textured draperies frame expansive windows, while Italian mosaics and oil paintings lend a touch of old-world sophistication. Bringing the opulence of the Gilded Age into the 21st century, the Del-Ray creates an ambiance where history and modernity meet. This exquisite setting serves as the perfect backdrop for savoring culinary masterpieces that have consistently earned an AAA Four-Diamond Award for two decades.

The experience at the Del-Ray is more than just a meal, it is an event. Live music floats down from the musicians' gallery above the restaurant during Friday and Saturday dinner service and Sunday brunch, adding a melodious charm to the atmosphere. For those hosting special occasions, the 4,000-square-foot restaurant and banquet hall provides a versatile space where dreams come to life, whether it is an intimate celebration or a grand gala.

The evening was alive with laughter and clinking glasses as guests gathered in the banquet hall. Amid the jubilant crowd, a series of sharp clangs echoed—a spoon striking a champagne flute. "Can I have your attention?" Bill's voice boomed over the hum of conversation. The room quieted, and all eyes turned toward him.

"Everyone," he began, "I just want to take a moment to say to Jane that the last 25 years we have been married have been incredible, and I cannot wait for twenty-five more. Here is to a happy wife and a happy life!"

Cheers erupted, and glasses were raised high in celebration. But as Bill lowered his champagne flute, his face turned pale. A sudden faintness overcame him, and he collapsed before Jane, friends, family, and the stunned staff. Chaos erupted. The room that had been filled with warmth and joy descended into a frenzy. Chairs scraped against the floor, tables overturned, and the shattering of glass punctuated the air. Amid the confusion, Jane's name was called repeatedly, a desperate plea cutting through the commotion.

"Jane, we need to go to the hospital!" someone urged, shaking her from her daze. As they hurried to the hospital, Jane's mind reeled back to the moment she first met Bill.

The Waiter and Mrs. Davis
By: Keith P. Mulrooney

It was a breezy October afternoon, the kind of day that painted the town in shades of amber and crimson. Sixteen-year-old Jane strolled past the Del-Ray, her scarf fluttering in the wind. Through the window, she caught sight of Bill—a tall, broad-shouldered young man of twenty, his brown hair tousled, and his crisp waiter's uniform neatly pressed. Their eyes met, and for a moment, time seemed to pause. The sunlight framed Jane in a golden glow, and as she smiled shyly, Bill felt an irresistible pull. Without hesitation, he dashed out of the café to introduce himself and get her phone number.

Their first date was at the annual fall festival, a vibrant tapestry of lights, laughter, and the sweet aroma of funnel cakes. They rode the Ferris wheel, their laughter mingling with the crisp night air. As the wheel ascended, Jane confided her dreams to Bill—her hopes, her ambitions, and the life she envisioned. When the wheel circled back around, Bill shared his own aspirations, and together they discovered a shared dream: to open a restaurant. As Jane placed her hand on his, a spark of electricity seemed to pass between them, sealing an unspoken promise.

As the weeks passed, Jane and Bill grew inseparable. Jane's hazel eyes would light up every time she saw Bill, and their bond deepened with each passing day. Her mother, however, was less than thrilled about the four-year age gap between them. Jane often found it amusing, knowing her parents shared the same difference in age, but she refrained from pushing the point.

Spring arrived, and Jane was nearing the end of her junior year of high school. Bill, now promoted to manager at the Del-Ray Café, was diligently learning all aspects of running the restaurant. His dream of opening his own establishment fueled his drive. That summer, Jane joined Bill at the café as a host, and together they immersed themselves in the intricate workings of the business.

One evening, after closing, Bill surprised Jane with a candlelit dinner of veal piccata and a dozen red roses. As she savored the meal, Bill leaned close, whispering sweet nothings that made her blush. Jane's feelings for Bill were growing stronger, and the sparks between them were undeniable. Afterward, they cleaned and locked up the café before walking hand in hand toward Jane's house.

The Waiter and Mrs. Davis
By: Keith P. Mulrooney

As they neared her home, Jane paused and asked Bill to take her to his place instead. Bill hesitated but agreed. He rented a room in a Cape Cod-style house on Oak Street, shared with Madison, a sharp-tongued but caring older woman. Madison had taken a liking to Bill, treating him like the son she never had. The house, with its weathered shutters and neatly landscaped yard, was quaint and charming despite its outdated interior.

Inside, the flickering glow of candles illuminated the living room, where Madison sat in her recliner watching *The Thorn Birds.*

"Bill," she called out.

"Yes," he replied.

"Can you take me to my doctor's appointment next week?" Madison demanded.

"Of course. I will adjust my schedule at the restaurant," Bill said warmly.

"Good boy," Madison muttered before noticing Jane. Her eyes narrowed in curiosity.

"Who's this young piece of meat?" Madison quipped.

"This is Jane, my girlfriend," Bill replied, exasperated.

"She looks young. Did you pick her up at the playground?" Madison retorted.

"I'm sixteen, ma'am," Jane interjected softly.

"Call me Madison, dear," she said, softening. "Bill is a good boy, very responsible. You have a keeper."

Later, in Bill's room—a cozy space adorned with green plaid wallpaper, a collection of Matchbox cars, and a small television—the two shared a tender moment. Their kiss was electric, but as emotions ran high, Jane suddenly pulled away. "I need to get home," she murmured, her voice trembling. Bill respected her wishes, walking her back without question.

The Waiter and Mrs. Davis
By: Keith P. Mulrooney

Days turned into weeks. At Madison's doctor's appointment, she was diagnosed with phlebitis—a blood clot in her leg that required rest and care. On their way out, they encountered Jane, hobbling on crutches.

"What happened?" Bill asked, his concern evident.

"Sprained it in gym class," Jane replied, smiling through the pain. Her mother, however, scowled at their interaction.

Madison, ever protective, snapped, "What is with the sour face? Can't you see they love each other?"

Jane's mother retorted, "He is too old for her and has not even gone to college. He is a loser!"

Madison fired back, "My last husband did not go to college, and he built the Del-Ray Restaurant in Montclair County into a success. Love matters more than credentials!"

Jane's mother stormed off, leaving Jane and Bill in stunned silence.

"I'm sorry about Madison," Bill began, but Jane interrupted, "She is right. My mom's judgmental, and it is not fair."

Their bond grew stronger that day, fortified by the challenges they faced together.

Chapter 2

Bill and Madison sat on the bleachers in the high school gym, the faint strains of "Pomp and Circumstance" playing softly through the speakers as graduates in caps and gowns filed into rows of white chairs. The air buzzed with anticipation, punctuated by the occasional murmur from the crowd and the rustle of programs. Sunlight streamed through the gym's high windows, illuminating the scene in a golden hue.

Madison's sharp eyes wandered and landed on Jane's mother, who was seated a few rows down, fussing with a compact mirror. "Look over there," Madison said, her tone dripping with sarcasm. "Your future snotty mother-in-law, trying to look all prim and proper."

Bill sighed heavily, running a hand through his dark hair. "Yup. She makes our relationship difficult."

"Forget her," Madison whispered, her words biting but quiet enough not to draw attention. Her expression softened slightly as she nudged Bill with her elbow. "You and Jane are solid. Do not let her mother get in the way."

Before Bill could respond, Madison's breathing hitched. Her hand flew to her chest as her face tightened with discomfort. "Are you okay, Madison?" Bill asked, his voice rising with concern.

"Yes… just feeling a heaviness in my chest," Madison replied faintly. But her breaths grew shallow, her complexion turning ashen. Panic flickered in Bill's eyes.

On the gym floor, the principal's voice boomed through the microphone. "Jane Winthorp!" The announcement was met with applause, but the joyous atmosphere was shattered as Madison suddenly slumped forward, collapsing onto the bleachers.

Gasps rippled through the audience as heads turned toward the commotion. "Call 911! Is there a doctor or nurse here?" Bill shouted, his voice cracking. He knelt beside Madison, gripping her hand tightly. His heart pounded as chaos erupted around them. Paramedics rushed in, their movements swift and precise as they worked to revive her.

From the gym floor, Jane glanced up, alarmed by the growing commotion. She spotted Bill, tears streaming down his face as he clung to Madison's hand. Without hesitation, Jane jumped from her seat and raced up the bleachers to his side. Her cap and gown fluttered as she climbed, her focus solely on Bill.

Jane's mother, initially horrified by the scene, observed her daughter's frantic reaction. For the first time, she glimpsed the depth of Jane and Bill's bond. Madison's words from the doctor's office echoed in her mind: "Love is the only thing you need." Something shifted in her heart.

The paramedics carefully placed Madison on a stretcher, continuing CPR as they wheeled her toward the ambulance. Bill and Jane followed closely in Madison's car, Jane still in her graduation attire. The silence between them was heavy with unspoken fears.

At the hospital, Jane's mother arrived with a change of clothes for her daughter. She approached Bill, who sat trembling in the waiting room, his head in his hands. Gently, she placed a hand on his shoulder. "I know how much my daughter loves you," she said softly. "I am only interested in what is best for her. I can see now how much she cares for you, and I give my blessing to your relationship."

Bill looked up; his face streaked with tears. "I love Jane with my whole heart," he said, his voice cracking. "I will never hurt her. I want to give her the world and spend the rest of my life with her."

Jane's mother, her own tears welling up, reached out to wipe his cheek. "I know you do. And I see now that you will."

Overwhelmed, Jane hugged her mother tightly, a moment of unity that felt long overdue.

Moments later, the doctor emerged, his expression somber. "Madison Churchill's family?" he called out.

Bill stood, dread pooling in his stomach. Jane clutched his arm as they followed the doctor to a private room.

"I'm very sorry," the doctor began, his voice gentle. "Ms. Churchill did not make it. She suffered a pulmonary embolism."

Bill sank into a chair, the weight of grief crashing over him like a tidal wave. Memories of his mother, whom he had lost at sixteen, resurfaced, intertwining with the pain of losing Madison. She had been his rock, his family, his guiding light. Jane knelt beside him; her arms wrapped tightly around his trembling frame. Her quiet strength anchored him in the storm of emotions.

Later that night, Bill sat alone in Madison's bedroom, the faint scent of her lavender perfume lingering in the air. He opened the small safe in her closet, finding her life insurance policy, bank information, and a meticulously written Last Will and Testament.

His hands shook as he unfolded the document and began to read:

Last Will and Testament
I, Madison Churchill, a legal resident of Montclair County, being over eighteen years of sound and disposing mind and memory, and not acting under duress or undue influence of anyone, do hereby make, publish, and declare this to be my Last Will and Testament, hereby revoking and making null and void all former Wills, Testaments, or Codicils at any time heretofore made by me.

FIRST: I name my adopted son, William Ray Davis, of Montclair County, as Executor of my Will, and I request that he be allowed to function as Executor without giving surety on his bond, conditioned upon the faithful performance of his duties.

SECOND: I direct my Executor to pay all my legal debts, funeral expenses, and any applicable taxes as an administration expense.

THIRD: I bequeath my fifty percent (50%) ownership of the Del-Ray to my adopted son, William Ray Davis.

FOURTH: I bequeath my house, vehicle, and all personal contents to my adopted son, William Ray Davis.

FIFTH: I give, devise, and bequeath $250,000 of my life insurance policy and $500,000 in checking, savings, stocks, and bonds to my adopted son, William Ray Davis.

SIXTH: The balance of my estate, including all real property, tangible assets, and residual wealth, shall be bequeathed entirely to William Ray Davis.

Bill's hands trembled as he finished reading. Madison had entrusted him with everything—her legacy, her life's work, her home. The magnitude of her love and belief in him was overwhelming.

As the night wore on, Bill found solace in Jane's unwavering presence. They sat together in his bedroom, the silence between them profound yet comforting.

Bill leaned over, planting a soft kiss on her temple. "I don't know what I'd do without you," he whispered.

"You'll never have to find out," Jane replied, her voice steady with resolve. "We'll get through this together."

Chapter 3

Two years later…

The sound of hammers and saws echoed through the air as construction on the new 2,000-square-foot banquet hall at Del-Ray neared completion. The once-humble restaurant was transforming into an elegant restaurant, with a banquet hall—as its crowning achievement. Bill had poured his heart and soul into this project, envisioning a space that would host weddings, banquets, and celebrations. Initially, Tom Churchill, Madison's ex-husband, resisted the idea, fearing it would erode the restaurant's small-town charm. But as inquiries poured in about the new venue, even Tom admitted the potential for success.

At home, Jane was busy planning her wedding to Bill, her hands fluttering over a stack of invitations. Suddenly, she felt a small movement in her abdomen—a tiny flutter that brought an immediate smile to her face.

"Okay, little one, I know you're hungry," Jane whispered, placing a hand on her growing belly. She had discovered her pregnancy a month ago, and she and Bill had just finished renovations in Madison's house, preparing for their future as a family.

That evening, Bill came home, his face alight with excitement. "The banquet hall will be done by the end of the month, just in time for our wedding," he announced. "We'll be the first to celebrate at Del-Ray Hall!"

Jane's eyes sparkled. "Don't forget we have our ultrasound appointment tomorrow," she reminded him with a grin.

The next morning, Bill and Jane arrived at the doctor's office; anticipation etched on their faces. The room was dimly lit, the hum of the ultrasound machine filling the air. Jane's heartbeat quickened as the doctor began, pointing out the tiny features on the screen.

"Here's the nose, the hand, and the feet," the doctor said warmly. Suddenly, he paused, moving the probe slightly.

"It seems there's another baby hiding back here," he added with a smile. "You're having twins!"

Bill's jaw dropped. "Twins?" he echoed, his voice a mix of shock and joy.

The doctor nodded. "Yes, and they're both girls."

Tears welled up in Jane's eyes as she looked at Bill, who was visibly overcome. "This is a miracle," he whispered, his voice thick with emotion.

That evening, Bill sat on the patio with a cold beer, the setting sun casting a warm glow over the yard. He reflected on how far he had come—from the tragic day he found his mother's lifeless body to the unwavering support Madison had given him, and finally, to the love and light Jane had brought into his life. Now, with the news of their twin daughters, he felt as though the final piece of his life's puzzle had fallen into place.

The banquet hall was completed on schedule, with its gleaming chandeliers and polished floors exuding an air of sophistication. Bill could not contain his pride as the building inspector gave the final approval. Even Tom, who had been skeptical of the project, acknowledged its potential.

"We've already got several inquiries," he admitted. "This place is going to put Montclair on the map."

Bill nodded. "We will offer catered packages, live music, and unforgettable experiences. This is not just a venue—it is where memories will be made."

The first event at Del-Ray's new Banquet Hall was Bill and Jane's wedding. The hall was adorned with fresh flowers and twinkling lights, transforming it into a fairytale setting. As the bridesmaids walked down the aisle to Pachelbel's Canon in D, Bill stood at the altar, his palms sweating but his smile unwavering. He glanced at the church doors, waiting for Jane to appear.

Jane's uncle approached her just outside the door. "Are you ready?" he asked gently.

The Waiter and Mrs. Davis
By: Keith P. Mulrooney

Jane took a deep breath. "Ready as I'll ever be," she replied, her voice trembling with emotion.

The doors opened, and the Bridal Chorus began. Jane stepped forward, her dress glistening in the soft light, her veil framing her radiant face. She scanned the room, her eyes locked with Bill's. Tears welled up as she saw the love and admiration in his gaze.

The priest led them through their vows, their voices steady despite the emotion thick in the air.

"I, Jane, take thee, William, to be my wedded husband, to have and to hold from this day forward, for better, for worse, for richer, for poorer, in sickness and in health, to love and to cherish, till death do us part."

"I, William, take thee, Jane, to be my wedded wife, to have and to hold from this day forward, for better, for worse, for richer, for poorer, in sickness and in health, to love and to cherish, till death do us part."

The priest smiled. "William, you may kiss your bride."

Bill lifted Jane's veil, his hands trembling. He leaned in, their lips meeting in a kiss that stopped time. The guests erupted to applause as the organ swelled with Mendelssohn's Wedding March. Hand in hand, Bill and Jane walked down the aisle, their hearts full of love and hope for the future.

As the reception began, laughter and music filled the hall. Jane's hand rested on her belly, a quiet reminder of the new life they were bringing into the world. Bill caught her gaze, his eyes shining with adoration.

"Here's to us," he said, raising his glass. "And to the adventure ahead."

Chapter 4

"Let's go!" Jane barely managed to speak through the searing pain as Bill rushed her into the hospital. They arrived just in time, securing the last available room: Room 44. The room had been untouched for over a year, its sterile, pristine condition almost unsettling. But for now, it was their refuge.

Doctor Bonner entered swiftly; his expression was grim. "We have a complication," he announced, scanning Jane's chart and ultrasound images. "One of the babies—her umbilical cord is wrapped around her neck."

Bill's face was drained of color. "What does that mean? Is she going to be, okay?"

Doctor Bonner met his gaze with calm but urgent determination. "We need to act immediately. There is no time. We will need to deliver her now to save her life."

Panic seized Jane as waves of pain crashed over her. "Get them out of me!" she screamed, clutching Bill's hand with all her strength. Her body felt as though it was being torn apart, and exhaustion threatened to consume her.

"Stay with me, Jane," Bill whispered, his voice shaking. "You are so strong. You can do this."

A nurse dabbed Jane's forehead with a cool cloth. "Breathe, Jane. Deep breaths. You are doing great."

Just then, the door opened, and Jane's mother hurried in. Her presence was a balm to Jane's frazzled nerves.

"Mom," Jane sobbed, tears streaming down her face.

Her mother moved to her side, gripping one of Jane's legs to help. "I am here, sweetheart. You have this. Just keep breathing."

Jane bores down with all her might, her screams echoing through the sterile room. "I can't do it!" she cried, her strength waning.

"Yes, you can," her mother encouraged. "One more push, Jane. For your babies."

Summoning every ounce of willpower, Jane gave one final, monumental push. The first baby's head emerged, and Doctor Bonner expertly untangled the umbilical cord before easing the tiny girl into the world. A piercing cry filled the room, and the baby was placed on Jane's chest.

"She's beautiful," Jane whispered through her tears, her heart swelling with love as she held her daughter close.

But there was no time to rest. Moments later, the second baby began to crown. The delivery was smoother this time, and within minutes, the second baby slid into the doctor's hands. Bill, tears streaming down his face, cut the cord and cradled the crying newborn in his arms.

"Two perfect girls," Doctor Bonner announced, a warm smile spreading across his face. "Congratulations, Mom and Dad."

Bill and Jane exchanged a tearful, joy-filled glance. "I love you," they said in unison, their voices thick with emotion.

"What should we name them?" Jane asked, her eyes never left the tiny faces of her daughters.

Bill chuckled, rattling off a few names. "Tiffany? Stephanie? Tabitha?"

Jane laughed softly. "No," she said, shaking her head. "Maddy, after Madison Churchill, and Maya."

Bill's expression softened. "Maddy and Maya Davis. Perfect."

The nurses took the babies for a few routine tests while Jane's mother held her hand, tears of pride streaming down her face. "You were amazing," she said, her voice trembling. "And now you have two beautiful daughters."

Doctor Bonner returned shortly after, his expression reassuring. "Both girls are healthy and doing just fine," he confirmed. Relief washed over the room like a gentle wave.

That night, Bill sat by Jane's hospital bed, one arm wrapped protectively around her as they gazed at their sleeping daughters in the basinet nearby. The room was quiet, safe for the soft hum of the monitors and the gentle breathing of their newborns.

"We did it," Jane whispered, her head resting on Bill's shoulder. "Our family is complete."

Bill kissed her temple, his heart overflowing with gratitude. "Here's to Maddy and Maya," he said softly, his voice brimming with emotion. "And to the rest of our lives together."

Together, they sat in peaceful silence, the weight of the day melting away as they embraced the joy and love that filled the room.

Chapter 5

The leaves on the trees were beginning to change, painting the town in vibrant hues of orange and red. It had been six months since Bill's passing, and the days felt both fleeting and endless for Jane. With Maddy and Maya away at Montclair University—Maddy studying to be a schoolteacher and Maya diving into history—Jane buried herself in the day-to-day operations of the restaurant. Del-Ray was bustling as it prepared to host the town's annual Strawberry Festival in the banquet hall.

To manage the influx of guests, Jane placed an ad in the Del-Ray Community College paper, seeking banquet servers for the event. The response was promising, and Jane soon found herself interviewing a variety of applicants. Among them was a young man who immediately stood out: Chip Urban. With dark hair, piercing blue eyes, and a rugged 5 o'clock shadow, he reminded Jane so much of a younger Bill that her breath caught.

Chip was polite and confident, his resume reflecting two years of experience as a waiter at a now-closed local diner. He was studying Culinary Arts and Hotel/Restaurant Management and had even attended the same high school as Jane's daughters, though he had not socialized with them. Jane saw potential in Chip—not just as a capable worker, but as someone she could mentor, continuing Bill's legacy of guiding the younger generation.

Dawn, the restaurant manager, interrupted Jane's musing with updates on the festival's decorations and activities. "Mayor McBride will be attending," Dawn added, raising an eyebrow.

The day of the Strawberry Festival arrived, bringing a crisp October breeze. The town turned out in full force, dressed in shades of red. Some wore strawberry-themed hats, and others wore bright red scarves. The streetlights were adorned with paper strawberries and garlands, and the Del-Ray banquet hall was transformed with red tablecloths and baskets of fresh strawberries at each table. The dessert table boasted an impressive array of strawberry pies, pretzels, and chocolate-dipped strawberries. Outside, children bounced gleefully in a strawberry-shaped bounce house and posed with a cheerful strawberry mascot.

Mayor McBride took to the microphone, her voice resonating through the crowd as she declared the start of National Strawberry Day. She spoke of Montclair's community spirit and announced her bid for re-election in November, earning a round of applause. With her speech concluded, the parade began, winding through the heart of town in a flurry of music and cheers.

As the parade ended, the festivities moved into the banquet hall. Guests mingled, sipping drinks and sampling desserts, while children engaged in games and crafts. Chip moved gracefully through the crowd, balancing a tray of soft drinks. Dawn followed behind him, offering trays of chocolate-covered strawberries. Laughter filled the air—until chaos struck.

Two children with water guns darted around the hall, giggling as they sprayed on each other. Chip attempted to intercept them, warning them about the slippery floor, but it was too late. Mayor McBride stepped onto a wet spot, her heel slipping out from under her. As she flailed for balance, Chip lunged to steady her. In the commotion, the dessert table wobbled and collapsed, sending an avalanche of strawberry pies crashing to the floor—and onto the Mayor and Chip.

For a moment, there was stunned silence. Then Mayor McBride burst into laughter. "Well, I can't say this isn't memorable!" she exclaimed, her suit stained with strawberry filling.

Chip, drenched and frustrated, forced a polite smile. "Glad you're okay, ma'am," he said, his cheeks as red as the strawberries.

Jane hurried over, her concern evident. "Chip, are you hurt?"

"Just my elbow," he admitted, rubbing it gingerly. "Nothing a little ice won't fix."

"There are clean shirts in my office. Change," Jane insisted, guiding him toward the back.

In Jane's office, Chip found a neatly folded white shirt. As he unbuttoned his soiled one, his gaze fell on a framed family photo on Jane's desk. He recognized Maya from high school and noted the strong resemblance between Bill and the daughters. The photo stirred something as a reminder of his own aspirations to build one day something as meaningful as the Del-Ray.

Just as he slipped on the fresh shirt, Jane walked in. They both froze, caught off guard.

"Oh! I am so sorry," Jane stammered, her cheeks flushing as she averted her eyes.

"It's okay, Mrs. Davis," Chip said with a sheepish grin. "I should've locked the door."

Jane lingered for a moment, her thoughts racing. Chip's youthful energy and striking resemblance to Bill stirred emotions she had not felt in years. Embarrassed, she muttered an apology and left the room, her heart pounding.

As the evening wound down, Chip helped clean the hall, his earlier frustration giving way to quiet determination. Mayor McBride approached him, her clothes now free of pie stains.

"Thank you for catching me," she said warmly. "You saved me from a far worse fall."

"Just doing my job, ma'am," Chip replied with a modest smile.

By the time the last decorations were packed away, Dawn stretched with a satisfied sigh. "Another successful festival in the books."

"Agreed," Jane said, her voice tinged with pride. "The mayor even mentioned wanting to host a Breakfast with Santa here in December…if she's reelected."

"If," Dawn echoed with a wry smile.

Chip bid them goodnight, declining Dawn's offer of a ride home. "I will walk. I need to clear my head," he said, his tone reflective.

Jane watched him go, her thoughts swirling. There was something special about Chip—something familiar and grounding. As she drove home, she could not help but think of Bill and the walks he would take after a long day to gather his thoughts. Chip's sincerity and kindness reminded her of a time when such qualities were more common.

At home, the stillness was almost unbearable. With Maddy and Maya gone, the house felt emptier than ever. Jane stepped into the bedroom she had shared with Bill and opened his closet, pulling out clothes to donate. As she folded his shirts, a wave of grief overcame her.

"Why did you leave me so early?" she whispered, tears streaming down her face. Hugging one of his flannels to her chest, she sank onto the bed, her sobs filling the silence of the empty house.

Chapter 6

It was a crisp autumn morning when Jane stood in her front yard, trimming the rose bushes. The sun shone brightly, casting a golden hue over the neighborhood, while birds sang cheerfully in the trees. Squirrels scurried about, gathering food for the coming winter. Jane knelt in the flowerbed, carefully laying mulch around the base of the bushes, savoring the calm.

A voice interrupted her thoughts. "Mrs. Davis?"

Startled, Jane looked up. Standing at the edge of her yard was a familiar figure. "Chip?" she exclaimed, surprised to see him. "What are you doing here?"

Chip shifted his weight, his hands tucked into his pockets. "I was out for a walk to clear my mind and thought I saw you from down the street. I didn't know you lived here."

Jane smiled warmly, brushing dirt off her gloves. "I've been here for years. What a small world! Where do you live?"

"Just two streets over, on Maple Street," Chip replied, his grin widening.

"Well, welcome to Oak Street," Jane said, chuckling. She glanced around her yard, noticing the scattered leaves. "This place is always a handful in the fall."

Chip's gaze followed hers. "Would you like some help? I could rake the leaves and bag them for you."

Jane hesitated for a moment, then nodded. "That would be wonderful! The rake and blower are in the shed out back. I'll grab some trash bags."

Chip quickly retrieved the tools and got to work, efficiently blowing leaves into neat piles and raking them into bags. Jane collaborated with him, feeling grateful for the company. Yard work had always been Bill's forte, and she had struggled to keep up since his passing. When they finished, she offered him a glass of lemonade.

"You've earned this," Jane said, handing him the drink. "And I would like to thank you properly. How about dinner tonight? My treat."

The Waiter and Mrs. Davis
By: Keith P. Mulrooney

Chip's eyes lit up. "That sounds great. Thank you, Mrs. Davis."

"Please, call me Jane," she insisted with a smile. "Come by at 7:30."

At 7:30 sharp, Chip arrived, looking sharp in grey slacks, a black button-down shirt, and a matching cardigan. Jane greeted him at the door, dressed in an elegant grey dress with a silver chain necklace and heels.

"Wow, don't you look handsome!" Jane said, her eyes twinkling.

Chip blushed. "Thank you, Jane. You look amazing."

Together, they drove to The Mills, a popular two-story restaurant in the heart of town. Nestled between a peaceful mosque and a lively entertainment club, the restaurant was known for its impeccable service and cozy ambiance. Inside, the white and brown checkered tiles gleamed under the soft lighting, and classical music played gently in the background.

They were seated in a quiet corner, and conversation flowed easily as they waited for their meals.

"So, what are your plans after college?" Jane asked, genuinely curious.

Chip's face brightened. "I am studying Culinary Arts and Hotel/Restaurant Management at Montclair Community College. One day, I want to open my own restaurant. Something warm and inviting, like Del Ray."

Jane's expression softened. "That is a wonderful dream, Chip. I am sure you will make it happen."

Encouraged, Chip shared more about his life. "I live with my Aunt Mary on Maple Street. My parents..." He hesitated, then continued. "They are divorced. My moms in Italy, and we do not talk much. My dad's in Honduras. He sends letters twice a year, but that is about it.

Jane reached across the table, touching his hand gently. "I am so sorry, Chip. That must be hard."

"It is sometimes, but Aunt Mary's great," he said, his voice tinged with both sadness and gratitude. "She works a lot, so I'm on my own most days."

"Well, if you ever feel lonely, you're welcome to visit me," Jane offered warmly. "My daughters are away at school, and since Bill…" Her voice faltered. "Let's just say the house gets too quiet."

Chip's smile was soft. "Thank you, Jane. I might take you up on that. And if you ever need help with the house, I am handy."

Their meals arrived, and the conversation continued over surf and turf for Jane and a cheeseburger for Chip. By the time dessert rolled around, Jane found herself enjoying Chip's company more than she had anticipated. For dessert, she ordered bananas foster, which was prepared flambé-style at their table. The flickering flames and rich aroma captivated them both.

"When I open my restaurant, this is definitely going on the menu," Chip said, grinning as he watched the syrupy bananas served over vanilla ice cream.

As they finished their meal, Jane could not ignore the spark she felt. It was subtle but undeniable, a warmth she had not experienced since Bill's passing. Whether it was the evening's charm or Chip's kindness, something had stirred within her.

Later that night, as Jane lay in bed, she reflected on the evening. Chip's youthful energy and ambition reminded her of herself at his age—and of Bill's steadfast determination. For the first time in months, she felt a glimmer of hope. The future held more than she'd dared to dream.

Chapter 7

The drive home from the restaurant was quiet, the kind of silence that felt natural after a delicious meal and an evening of connection. Jane and Chip sat comfortably, the car radio playing softly in the background. "Hungry Eyes" by Eric Carmen filled the air, its familiar melody stirring emotions neither of them expected.

Jane glanced at Chip, who seemed deep in thought. His eyes flickered toward her briefly, and she caught the faintest hint of a smile. For the first time in years, Jane felt something she could not name—a mix of curiosity and anticipation.

As they pulled into her driveway, Jane turned off the engine and looked at Chip. "Do you want me to drop you off at home, or would you like to come in for a bit?" she asked casually, though her heartbeat faster than she cared to admit.

Chip hesitated for a moment before replying. "If it is okay with you, I would like to stay and talk. The house feels empty when my aunt's not home."

Jane nodded, her lips curving into a warm smile. "Of course. Come in."

Inside, the house was quiet, saved for the faint hum of the refrigerator and the occasional creak of the floorboards. The scent of cinnamon lingered in the air, a comforting reminder of the fall season. Jane led Chip into the family room and gestured to the couch. "Make yourself comfortable. I will grab us some drinks."

Chip settled onto the couch, his eyes wandering around the room. Through the sliding glass door, he noticed the hot tub on the deck, its cover slightly ajar, and the soft glow of string lights casting a warm halo over the space. He had never been in a house quite like Jane's, it felt lived-in yet elegant, a reflection of her personality.

Jane returned with two glasses of wine. She handed one to Chip and sat beside him, closer than he expected. They sipped their drinks, the conversation starting light but gradually delving deeper—dreams, regrets, and the little moments that shaped their lives. Time seemed to blur.

When Chip excused himself to use the bathroom, Jane found herself wandering to the deck. The night was cool but pleasant, and the idea of soaking in the hot tub was tempting. On impulse, she decided to indulge. She retrieved a towel from the laundry room, removed the hot tub cover, and turned the jets on low. As the water began to bubble, she slipped out of her clothes and into the steaming water, sighing as the warmth enveloped her.

Chip returned to the family room, looking for Jane. When he glanced out the glass door, he saw her in the hot tub, her silhouette illuminated by the soft glow of the string lights. For a moment, he hesitated, unsure if he should join her.

Jane noticed him standing at the door. "It's so relaxing," she said, her voice carrying a playful edge. "You can join me if you'd like."

"I don't have anything to wear," Chip admitted, his cheeks flushing.

Jane chuckled. "Boxers will do just fine."

Chip's hesitation melted away as he kicked off his shoes and pulled off his shirt. He stepped out onto the deck, the cool night air brushing against his skin. Jane watched him with a mix of curiosity and admiration. As he climbed into the hot tub, the tension between them seemed to thicken, though neither spoke of it.

They sat side by side, the water swirling gently around them. The conversation resumed, but now it felt different, charged with an unspoken energy. At one point, Jane leaned back against the edge, her eyes drifting shut. Chip watched her, taking in the way the soft light played across her features. She looked peaceful, radiant even.

"What's on your mind, Chip?" Jane asked suddenly, her eyes were still closed.

Chip hesitated. "I was just thinking how... relaxed you look. It is nice to see you like this."

Jane opened her eyes and turned to him, a faint smile on her lips. "It has been a while since I have felt this way. Thank you for tonight. It has been lovely."

Before he could respond, Jane reached out, placing a hand on his. The gesture was simple but electric. Chip's heart raced, and he found himself leaning closer, drawn to her in a way he could not explain.

"Jane," he began, his voice barely above a whisper, "I…"

But words failed him as Jane shut down the distance between them, her lips brushing against him in a tentative kiss. For a moment, time stood still. Then, as if a dam had broken, the kiss deepened, and all the unspoken feelings between them poured out.

The night unfolded in a way neither had anticipated, their connection growing stronger with every shared touch and whispered word. It was not just about passion; it was about two people finding solace in each other, healing wounds they had not realized were still raw. By the time, the first rays of dawn peeked over the horizon, Jane and Chip lay tangled together, the world outside forgotten.

As they drifted to sleep, a single thought lingered in Jane's mind: for the first time in years, she felt truly alive.

Chapter 8

The afternoon light filtered softly through the windows as Jane and Chip worked together to get the house ready for Maddy and Maya's arrival. Jane moved through each room with purpose, making sure the beds were made, and everything was in its place. Chip, on the other hand, seemed content rearranging the furniture and taking care of the tiny details Jane had nearly forgotten. They had a rhythm together, a silent understanding that worked.

"I think we're just about ready," Jane said as she straightened a picture frame on the living room wall. "The girls will be here in a few hours."

Chip, standing in the doorway with a hammer in hand, nodded and wiped his brow. "It is looking great. But do you know what? I think we both deserve a break."

Jane smiled at the suggestion. She had been so focused on making everything perfect that she had not thought about stepping away for a bit. "A break sounds nice," she agreed.

Chip grinned. "How about Del Ray? we can grab a quiet lunch before everything gets hectic again."

The waitstaff brought over menus and a bottle of sparkling water, setting it between them. But neither Jane nor Chip seemed in any rush to open their menus. Instead, they learned in slightly, the space between them charged with an unspoken tension.

"So," Jane began, her voice quieter than usual. "What do you think the girls will make of all this?" She gestured to the house in her mind, the preparations that had taken over the past few days.

Chip shrugged, though his eyes sparkled with amusement. "I think they will love it. It has all been for them, after all."

They locked their eyes, and for a moment, everything else seemed to fade away. It was easy to forget the bustling world outside, easy to forget the impending arrival of Maddy and Maya. In this quiet, shared space, there was only the moment between them.

The Waiter and Mrs. Davis
By: Keith P. Mulrooney

As the waiter returned to take their orders, Chip gave a distracted nod, still looking at Jane. His hand reached across the table, brushing lightly over hers. Jane felt the heat of his touch before she realized he was moving closer, his face coming nearer to hers.

"Chip," she whispered, half in warning, half in invitation.

But he was already there, his lips brushing her softly at first, assessing the waters. The brief, tender kiss ignited something deeper in both. The warmth of the restaurant, the familiarity of their shared history, and the quiet tension between them created a moment that felt both dangerous and exhilarating.

Jane's heart raced as she felt herself giving into the kiss, her hand gripping his for support as the world around them disappeared. The kiss deepened, the kind that held promises, neither of them were quite ready to speak aloud, but both were more than willing to explore.

Suddenly, the sound of the restaurant door opening broke through the intimacy of the moment. Both instinctively pulled away, their breath coming in short gasps. Jane's cheeks flushed with embarrassment as she sat up straight, and Chip quickly ran a hand through his hair, trying to regain some composure.

Just then, Maddy stepped through the door, her eyes scanning the room. Her gaze flicked to their table, and the surprise that washed over her was impossible to miss. Maddy froze in place, staring at Jane and Chip for what felt like an eternity. Jane's heart skipped a beat.

"Maddy!" Jane exclaimed; her voice was shaky. "I—uh—we weren't expecting you just yet."

Maddy blinked a few times; clearly taken aback by the scene she had walked in on. Her lips twitched in what could have been a smirk, and for a moment, there was an awkward silence between them.

"Sorry, didn't mean to interrupt," Maddy said, her voice laced with a dry humor. She shifted her gaze from Jane to Chip and back again, taking in their disheveled, flushed appearances.

Chip, always quick on his feet, cleared his throat and leaned back in his chair. "I, uh, guess the timing was a bit off," he said with a half-chuckle, though his face was still flushed.

Maddy raised an eyebrow. "A little off?" She scanned the restaurant, noticing the soft light, the candle between them, and the intimate setting. Her smirk widened, and she could not resist teasing them a little. "Well, looks like I came at the right time."

Jane felt herself shrink in her seat, her face burning with embarrassment. She opened her mouth to respond, but Maddy spoke first, her tone turning serious in an instant.

"I did not mean to make it awkward. I just did not expect to find you two… like that."

"We weren't… doing anything too crazy," Jane said quickly, her voice faltering under Maddy's gaze.

Chip gave a shrug, trying to ease the tension. "It is fine, Maddy. Really. We were just—well, you know—taking a moment."

Maddy's expression softened as she nodded, her teasing tone fading. "I get it. Just… do not go making this a habit, all right? I cannot unsee that."

Jane laughed nervously, and Chip joined in, his deep laugh echoing in the quiet of the booth.

"Well," Maddy said, turning toward the entrance, "I will leave you two to your lunch. Maya's looking for me."

As she walked away, Jane and Chip exchanged an incredulous glance, their hearts still racing from the unexpected interruption.

"Well," Chip said, shaking his head with a grin, "that was definitely… something."

Jane let out a breath she did not realize she had been holding. "Yeah, something."

Chapter 9

The next day, Jane sat at the kitchen table, her hands wrapped around her coffee mug, her gaze distant as she fought back tears. "I've been seeing Chip Urban for the past month," she began, her voice trembling. "He's been helping me out around the restaurant and the house."

Chip stood by the counter, his posture stiff, unsure of what to do with himself. His mind raced, his thoughts muddled, as the weight of the situation pressed down on him. He had not expected this confrontation, and now, with Maddy in the room, he had no idea how to explain his relationship with Jane.

Maddy's voice cut through the silence, filled with disbelief. "Chip Urban? Of all people, he is my age! I went to high school with him!" she exclaimed, her mind struggling to process the situation.

"Yes, dear. He is twenty-one, an adult," Jane replied, trying to remain calm despite the whirlwind of emotions inside her.

"I know this might seem strange," Jane continued, her voice cracking, "but we fell in love. He has been there for me in ways no one else has, especially since your father passed." She wiped away a tear that had slipped down her cheek.

Maddy's face twisted in anger, and her arms crossed tightly over her chest. "I cannot believe this, Mom! He is just a kid!" she yelled, her voice rising with frustration.

Maddy's gaze flicked to Chip, who had begun fidgeting, clearly uncomfortable under the weight of her glare. "Chip Urban," she said, her voice laced with fury. "Why would you take advantage of my mother like this? She is vulnerable, still grieving the loss of my father."

Chip swallowed hard, trying to steady his nerves. "Look, I started helping your mom around the restaurant, and she has been helping me with my work-study for college. I started doing things around the house—fixing stuff, painting, yard work… and then, feelings just started to develop. It was not something I planned; it just happened."

Maddy's anger flared hotter. "Feelings? How about I give you a taste of what I am feeling right now, Chip? A punch in the face!" she screamed, her fists clenched.

"Stop, Maddy!" Jane intervened; her voice strained. She stood, moving closer to her daughter. "Please, let him explain."

"I can't process this right now, Mom!" Maddy shouted, her hands shaking. "You and Chip... in the restaurant office... I saw him... I saw everything!" Her voice cracked as the realization hit her fully.

"I need to get out of here," Maddy cried, her body trembling. "I'm going to stay at Tiffany's house tonight to try and process this!" Without another word, she turned and stormed out of the room.

"Okay, dear. Can we talk tomorrow?" Jane called after her, her voice breaking as she wiped away more tears.

Maddy did not respond, her footsteps echoing down the hallway as she left. Jane collapsed back into the chair, sobbing. Chip rushed to her side, wrapping his arms around her, holding her close.

"It'll be okay, Jane," Chip whispered gently, his own voice thick with emotion. "I love you. We will get through this."

As Jane clung to him, her heart ached. She knew Maddy had always been fiery, but it did not make this any easier. She had seen it coming, but now, in the aftermath of the confrontation, it felt like a tidal wave crashing over her.

It was Thanksgiving Day, and Jane had worked all morning to turn the house into a festive holiday haven. The smell of turkey and pumpkin pies filled the air, and the warmth of the season had managed to push through the tension that still lingered from the morning's confrontation. Maya was home from college, but she still did not know about Jane's relationship with Chip. Maddy had agreed to come for dinner but was still staying at Tiffany's house. Chip, meanwhile, was spending Thanksgiving with his aunt and other relatives. Jane had hoped that Maddy would not share the news with Maya just yet, giving her time to prepare for the conversation she needed to have.

The Waiter and Mrs. Davis
By: Keith P. Mulrooney

Jane finished setting the table, adjusting the silverware exactly right. As she did, the door opened, and Maya walked in, her bright smile a welcome sight.

"Hi, Maya! Happy Thanksgiving!" Jane said her tone warm but laced with the nerves she still could not shake.

"Hi, sweetie! I am so glad you are here! I have missed you both so much!" Maya replied, her eyes sparkling with excitement.

They shared a hug, and the three of them settled down to enjoy wine, cheese, and grapes while the turkey continued to cook. Maya filled Jane in on her college life, recounting the challenges of keeping up with coursework and managing her social life. Jane listened attentively, thankful for the brief respite of normalcy. But she knew that the conversation she had been avoiding had to happen. She needed to tell Maya about Chip.

Taking a deep breath, Jane steadied herself. "Girls, I need to talk to you about something serious. I have been seeing someone, and it has become a real relationship."

Maya looked at her with curiosity, while Maddy crossed her arms, still clearly upset.

"I am seeing someone special. His name is Chip Urban. He is twenty-one, and he went to high school with both of you. He has been helping me around the restaurant and the house, and we have really connected. He lives two blocks away with his aunt, and he is studying Culinary Arts and Hotel/Restaurant Management at Montclair Community College. I am even his work-study sponsor. This was not something I planned, but it just happened. And I am happy. I just need your support," Jane explained, her voice steady despite the lump in her throat.

Maya's eyes widened with recognition. "Chip? Isn't he that guy who was in a few of your classes, Maddy?"

"Yeah," Maddy replied reluctantly, her tone filled with hesitation.

"Well, he's young, but if he makes you happy, then go for it, Mom," Maya said, offering a tentative but genuine smile of support.

Maddy, still upset, was not as ready to offer her approval. "Well, Maya, you do not know the whole story. Last week, I saw Chip and Mom in her office at the restaurant. And... I saw things I can never unsee." Maddy's arms remained crossed, her face scrunched in frustration.

"Mom, why Chip? He is the same age as us. You were with him... after Dad..." Maddy's voice cracked, and Jane could see the pain in her daughter's eyes as she tried to process the emotions swirling inside her.

"I understand you're upset, Maddy," Jane said gently, her own heart aching. "But it is my life. Since your father passed, I have been lonely. I did not go looking for love; it just happened. And I acted on my feelings."

Maddy was silent for a moment, her gaze downcast, as if weighing everything Jane had said. "I don't know what to think, but I guess... if he treats you well, I can accept it." She sighed, her voice softening. "But, Mom, please... keep that stuff private. Not in the restaurant office," she added with a faint smirk.

Jane smiled faintly, grateful that Maddy was willing to accept it. "Thank you, Maddy. I am glad we can talk about this."

As the dinner preparations continued, the three of them shared stories about Bill, remembering the family traditions they still held dear. Jane's heart ached as she gazed at the empty chair at the end of the table—the one where Bill would have sat.

"Why didn't you invite Chip to dinner, Mom?" Maya asked, her voice thoughtful.

"He's with his aunt and other family members," Jane replied. "And honestly, I wanted our first Thanksgiving with just the three of us since your father passed. It has been a lot to process."

Maya nodded, understanding. "Can we go pick out our Christmas tree tomorrow?" she asked, breaking the quiet moment.

"Of course," Jane replied, the tradition still something she wanted to hold on to. It was a part of Bill that she wanted to keep alive, for as long as she could.

Chapter Ten

Two weeks had passed since Thanksgiving, and Jane's worry had only deepened. Chip, the young man who had brought a spark back into her life, had completely stopped communicating. No phone calls, no texts, no words at all. She had tried reaching out to him—three times a day, sometimes more, leaving messages full of concern—but every effort was met with silence. The deafening quiet was beginning to take a toll on her. Even Maya, sensing Jane's growing anxiety, had gone to Chip's aunt's house in search of him, but there was no sign of him anywhere.

Jane's mind raced with the worst possibilities. Had something happened to him? Or had he simply decided to walk away from everything, including her? This was not like Chip. Everyone at the restaurant knew how dependable and steady he was. He would not just disappear. And yet, his absence made her feel like she was drowning in uncertainty.

Days dragged on, and with each passing hour, Jane felt herself slipping into a deepening sense of dread. The weight of his disappearance was crushing. She could hardly get through the day without spiraling into darker thoughts. She could not bear to let go of the hope that something might break the silence.

Unable to shake the feeling that something was terribly wrong, Jane made the difficult decision to contact the local sheriff's office. She reported Chip missing, recounting every detail of which she could think. The sheriff took down her information and promised to open a case. But as the days continued to drag on without a word, and no new leads emerged, Jane began to feel hopeless.

Then, on a Sunday afternoon, something unexpected happened. Jane was sitting alone in the living room, exhausted from weeks of worry, and waiting. Maya had been doing her best to keep Jane's spirits up, but even she was beginning to show the strain. Maddy, meanwhile, had been lending a hand with the investigation, trying to help wherever she could, though it did little to ease the growing tension in the house. Jane had just started to gather the strength to face another day when, without warning, the door swung open.

Chip, of all people, hobbled into the room.

His appearance nearly stopped Jane's heart. He was on crutches, a bandage wrapped around his head, and his face was pale and strained. But the moment their eyes met; relief surged through her in a wave so strongly it nearly knocked her off her feet. Tears welled up in her eyes, and before she knew it, she was rushing toward him.

"Oh, honey, I'm so happy to see you!" Jane cried, her voice thick with emotion, her arms wrapping around him in a desperate hug.

Chip managed a weak, but genuine smile. "I am sorry, Jane. I am so sorry. I did not mean to worry about you. My phone... it was lost in the accident, and I could not reach anyone. I did not know how to contact you."

Maddy, who had been standing in the hallway, froze when she saw Chip. She took in his injuries, the crutches, the way his eyes were filled with sorrow and apology. And then, she noticed the way Jane's face lit up when she saw him—something deeper than just concern, something more like love.

For the first time, Maddy's guarded stance softened, and she saw the bond between Jane and Chip in a new light. It was not just a fleeting attraction. There was a genuine connection between them, something real. And it reminded her, however painfully, of the way her parents had once been.

Jane quickly helped Chip sit down on the couch, her hands shaking slightly as she guided him. "Sit down, please. Tell me everything. Maya, could you grab us something to drink? Some pie from the fridge?"

Maya nodded and went into the kitchen, while Jane sat down next to Chip, her heart racing with relief but also a nagging fear of what he might reveal.

Chip took a deep breath before speaking. "I am so sorry, Jane. I never meant for any of this to happen. The truth is... my aunt and I were in a head-on collision on our way to my uncle's house on Thanksgiving. The other car crossed the median and hit us. My aunt... she did not make it. I was in the hospital for three days before I could even think straight."

Jane's heart broke for him as he spoke, her hand instinctively reaching out to hold him. She glanced up as Maya returned, placing drinks and pie in front of her, sensing that the conversation would be heavy.

Chip's voice cracked as he continued, his eyes moistening. "After that, I stayed at my uncle's house. We had to plan my aunt's funeral, and now... now he is selling the house. I do not even know where I am going to go next. I am lost."

The words hung in the air between them, and Jane felt an overwhelming urge to help. Without a second thought, she looked at him with determination in her eyes.

"You're coming to live with me," she said, her voice firm yet gentle. "I have an extra room, Chip. You're welcome to stay with me as long as you need. You have been through so much, and I am not letting you face this alone."

Chip hesitated, a mixture of gratitude and uncertainty flashing across his face. "Are you sure? I do not want to be a burden to you."

Jane smiled softly, her expression warm. "You are not a burden, Chip. I have the space, and you have been there for me through everything. I want to be there for you, too."

Chip managed a small grin, though his eyes were still filled with sadness. "Well, maybe I'd rather stay in your bedroom..." he teased, his attempt at lightening the mood a small spark of warmth.

Jane chuckled, a moment of levity. "In time, sweetheart. In time..."

The next day, Jane packed up some boxes from the restaurant and drove Chip to his aunt's house. As they sorted through his belongings, Jane watched him carefully. His face was etched with pain as he sifted through old photos and mementos of his aunt. The grief was raw and unfiltered. Jane stood beside him, offering a quiet kind of support. She could relate to his loss, having gone through her own grief in the wake of Bill's passing. The pain was familiar, but, just maybe, they could help each other heal.

At home, Maddy's reaction to Chip moving in was far from enthusiastic. She had always been fiercely protective of Jane, especially after losing her father. The thought of her mother opening her home to someone so young, someone who was so involved in their lives, made her uncomfortable. She struggled to understand the depth of the relationship between Jane and Chip, and she was not sure she was ready to accept it.

Still, Jane stood firm. "It's my life, Maddy," she said quietly, her voice soft but unwavering. "It's my heart, and I'm doing what feels right for me."

Chip began to recover physically, and despite his ongoing grief, he threw himself into his work at the restaurant, picking up extra shifts in preparation for Christmas. He wanted to buy Jane something special gift that would show her just how much he appreciated everything she had done for him.

As Christmas drew closer, the house filled with the warmth and joy of the holiday season. Maya and Maddy had decorated the restaurant, honoring the family tradition that had begun when Bill was still alive. This year, the familiar decorations seemed even more important, a way to hold on to the past while embracing the future.

But Christmas Eve at the restaurant turned chaotic in an instant. A loud argument broke out between four patrons at a corner table. At first, it seemed like a minor disturbance, but Chip, always alert, saw the tension escalate. Without warning, one of the women grabbed a knife from the table and stabbed one of the men in the neck.

Shock rippled through the room. Another woman, acting in self-defense, grabbed a second knife and stabbed the original attacker. Screams filled the air as the customers scrambled to escape. The restaurant, once a place of celebration, descended into a panic. Chip stayed calm, trying to manage the chaos, directing people to safety where he could.

Within minutes, the sirens of approaching ambulances and police cars pierced the air. By the time they arrived, most of the customers had fled, many leaving without paying for their meals. The holiday atmosphere had been shattered in an instant.

Despite the tragic turn of events, Chip remained determined to stay strong for Jane. He was looking forward to spending Christmas with her, to starting a new chapter in their lives, and to building a future together, no matter what obstacles they would face.

Chapter 11

It was Christmas morning, and Chip's mind was still heavy with the traumatic events from the night before. The violence at the restaurant was something he could not shake, and the thought of having to give a statement to the sheriff's office the next day only added to the weight on his shoulders. The terror and chaos from the evening haunted him. How was he supposed to move forward after that? But as he poured himself a cup of coffee and walked over to Jane in the kitchen, he knew he had to try.

Jane, ever the optimist, was in the kitchen preparing breakfast. She was trying to keep the day as normal as possible, hoping the comfort of a warm meal would help distract them all from the emotional rollercoaster of the past few days. As Chip kissed her gently on the cheek, she smiled at him, trying to gauge how he was really feeling.

"You are doing okay, hon?" she asked, noticing the faraway look in his eyes.

Chip sighed, rubbing his temples. "I will be fine. Just still shaken up by last night."

Before they could talk further, Maddy and Maya stumbled into the kitchen, still bleary-eyed from sleep. Maya immediately went for the cinnamon rolls Jane had baked, while Maddy poured herself a cup of coffee, her eyes darting to Chip, trying to read him.

"The breakfast casserole will be ready in about fifteen minutes," Jane remarked as she checked the oven.

"I love your fresh cinnamon rolls, Mom!" Maya said, her mouth full of pastry.

"Yeah, we heard about what happened last night at the restaurant," Maya added, looking at Chip. "What exactly went down?"

"Yeah, I heard it all over the police radio," Maddy chimed in. Her casual tone was laced with concern, especially since her boyfriend was a local police officer and had briefed her on the situation.

Chip and Jane exchanged a glance, the weight of the night's events hanging between them. They began to recount the harrowing events of the previous evening—the argument between patrons, the stabbing, the chaos that ensued. Just as they finished, the timer on the oven went off, signaling that the breakfast casserole was ready.

As Jane bent down to pull it from the oven, a sudden dizziness hit her. She swayed, and before anyone could react, she fainted, collapsing toward the floor.

In a split second, Chip was by her side, catching her just in time. His heart raced as he gently lowered her onto the couch, his mind a whirlwind of worry. He called out for Maya to bring some water, and within moments, the family had gathered around Jane, who began to stir.

"Mom?" Maya called softly, worried evident in her voice.

Jane's eyes fluttered open, her vision blurry. She whispered softly, "I don't feel right, Chip."

"Do not worry, Jane. We are getting you checked out," Chip said, his voice full of tenderness as he kissed her hand and rubbed her forehead comfortingly.

The next thing Jane knew, she was being carefully lifted into an ambulance, Chip by her side, Maddy and Maya following in Jane's car. Jane, still disoriented, murmured, "I don't feel like myself, Chip."

"We're going to get you the help you need," Chip reassured her, holding her hand tightly.

At the hospital, Jane rushed into a room where doctors immediately began running tests. They hooked her up to an IV to administer fluids, and for two long hours, Chip and the others waited in tense silence.

Finally, the doctor entered the room, his expression serious but compassionate. "We've run a number of tests, Mrs. Davis," he began, his voice soft. "One of the tests came back abnormal."

A chill settled in the room, and Jane's heart began to race. Maddy, Maya, and Chip all exchanged anxious glances, bracing themselves for what would come next.

"Mrs. Davis... you're pregnant."

"PREGNANT?!" Jane gasped, the word echoing in her mind as her body went numb with shock.

"Pregnant?!" Maddy echoed, her voice filled with disbelief.

Chip slumped back in his chair, stunned by the news. His mind reeled as he tried to process the unexpected revelation.

"How could this happen?" Jane whispered, still in shock, her mind spinning.

Maddy, attempting to lighten the mood, quipped, "Well, Mom, you did have sex. Remember the birds and the bees talk?" But the humor did not land. The tension in the room was too heavy.

Maya, her eyes bright with excitement, added, "I hope it is a boy! I always wanted a brother!"

Maddy shot Maya a look, clearly not the time for that comment, but Maya was too excited to hold back.

Jane, still reeling from the news, turned to the doctor. "I know my cycle's been irregular, and I thought I was just going through menopause..."

The doctor nodded sympathetically. "Even with irregular cycles, conception is still possible. You should make an appointment with your OB-GYN as soon as possible. Being pregnant at an older age can present complications."

The doctor's words hit Jane like a ton of bricks, and the weight of the situation settled on her chest. She remained calm, though. "Thank you, Doctor. Merry Christmas," she said softly, her voice steady despite the chaos inside her.

The Waiter and Mrs. Davis
By: Keith P. Mulrooney

As the nurse came in with Jane's discharge papers and unhooked the IV, the family stood in stunned silence, each person trying to process the reality of what had just happened.

Back at home, Maya began preparing Christmas dinner so Jane could rest, while Chip offered to help. The news of the pregnancy hung heavily in the air, but they also began discussing the future. Chip, still in shock, vowed that he would be present for their child in a way that his own father never had been. It was a promise he would keep.

Later that evening, Maddy came into Jane's room with a cup of hot tea, her face still carrying the weight of their earlier conversation. She tucked Jane in with a blanket, but despite the tension, Jane felt surrounded by love and care.

"Mom, what are you going to do?" Maddy asked quietly, her voice filled with concern.

Jane, still lost in her thoughts, responded, "About what?"

"The baby, Mom… What are you going to do about it?" Maddy pressed, her tone shifting toward anxiety.

Jane looked at her daughter and, with a steady voice, replied, "I'm going to have it, of course."

Maddy, trying to hide her concern, exploded, "But, Mom, you are older! The doctor said there could be complications!"

Jane sighed deeply. "There can be complications with any pregnancy, Maddy. I have thought it through."

The tension between them boiled over, and soon the argument escalated.

"Maddy, get out of my house!" Jane shouted, her voice raw with emotion. "I do not need this right now. You have been nothing but unsupportive of my decisions."

Maddy, hurt and angry, snapped back, "Since Dad passed, you have been acting like a teenager! You need to get it together, Mom!"

The Waiter and Mrs. Davis
By: Keith P. Mulrooney

"GET OUT!" Jane screamed, finally breaking down under the weight of the day.

Maddy stormed out, slamming the door behind her. Jane collapsed onto the bed, sobbing uncontrollably. Maya and Chip rushed to her side, doing their best to offer comfort and solace.

"Mom, she's been awful since Thanksgiving," Maya said softly, her frustration clear.

Chip put a reassuring hand on Jane's shoulder. "I am here for you, Jane. I am not going anywhere."

The rest of the day passed quietly. Maya and Chip finished preparing Christmas dinner—spiral honey ham, green bean casserole, whole baby potatoes, and apple pie for dessert. Despite her exhaustion, Jane managed to enjoy the meal they prepared, feeling the love from those around her.

"We still haven't opened presents," Jane remarked, a small smile tugging at her lips.

"We can do that after we clean up, if you're up for it," Chip said, smiling back.

"Yes, that sounds great," Maya agreed.

After dinner, Chip cleared the table, washing dishes, while Maya packed up leftovers. Jane retreated to the living room, where she settled onto the couch, turning on the fireplace. Chip and Maya chatted about the baby, with Maya excited about the idea of a brother, and Chip reaffirming his commitment to being a father to the child, vowing not to repeat the mistakes of his own father.

Later, Chip handed Maya her present—a beautiful scarf and gloves set with a matching wallet. Maya beamed with excitement, hugging him tightly in thanks.

Then, Chip presented Jane with her gifts—a diamond necklace with matching earrings, a silk robe with slippers, and her favorite perfume. Jane's eyes sparkled with joy as she hugged him tightly, overwhelmed with emotion.

The Waiter and Mrs. Davis
By: Keith P. Mulrooney

Maya gave Jane a thoughtful gift—a lovely antique picture frame, a subscription to her favorite magazine, a leather jacket, and a candle. Jane was deeply touched by the thoughtfulness.

"I feel so blessed, so loved, this Christmas," Jane said, her heart full of gratitude.

Finally, Jane handed Maya her gift—a quilt made from Maya's old hoodie sweaters, with a picture of Maya and Bill sewn into the fabric. Maya broke down in tears as she opened it.

"Mom, this is the best present I've ever gotten," Maya said, her voice thick with emotion.

"I'm so happy you love it, dear," Jane replied, holding her daughter close.

Jane then handed Chip his gift—a hooded sweatshirt, sweatpants, and cologne.

"Thank you, babe!" Chip said, pulling her into a tight hug.

"You're welcome, sweetie," Jane whispered. "You've already given me the best Christmas present of all."

As they all settled in, the wrapping paper scattered across the floor, Chip brought in some tea and apple pie. He looked around at the family he had found—one filled with love, hope, and support.

"Despite everything we've been through this year, this has been one of the best Christmases I've ever had," Chip said, his voice full of gratitude. "And I'm so glad to spend it with all of you—the people I care about the most."

In that moment, they all knew that no matter what challenges lay ahead, they could face them together, as a family.

Chapter 12

The day after Christmas, Chip went to the police station to give his statement about the events that unfolded at the Del-Ray on Christmas Eve. The meeting was long, lasting two hours. The detectives asked him a series of questions, digging deeper into the incident. Chip's mind raced as he tried to recall every detail of the shocking night. The questions made him feel uneasy, the trauma of what happened still fresh in his mind. The detectives informed him that they would be conducting a final sweep of the restaurant before he, Jane, and Maya could return to clean it up.

When Chip returned home, he found Jane sitting at the kitchen table, looking contemplative. She had already decided it was best to keep the restaurant closed until the New Year. The series of events, the terrifying incident at the restaurant, her fainting on Christmas morning, and the surprise pregnancy—had left her emotionally and physically drained. Plus, she wanted her staff to spend time with their families. It was not an easy decision, but Jane knew it was the right one for her peace of mind.

While Chip was at the station, he ran into Maddy. She was visiting her boyfriend, Jeff, who had recently joined the Montclair County Police Force. Maddy seemed a little uneasy as she approached Chip, her face filled with remorse.

"I'm really sorry for how I acted yesterday," Maddy said, her voice sincere.

Chip sighed, still processing the chaotic few days. "It's not me you need to apologize to, Maddy. It is your mother. She needed you yesterday, and you turned against her. She's vulnerable right now, especially after everything—the restaurant incident, passing out on Christmas morning, and then the pregnancy news."

Maddy lowered her gaze, visibly ashamed. "I know. I have been all over the place since Dad passed. I never thought I would have to share Mom with anyone, let alone someone so close to my age. Chip, do you understand that?"

Chip nodded, understanding the complicated emotions Maddy was grappling with. "I get it. My aunt was not thrilled when I first told her about your mom and me. She said, 'If she makes you happy and you get butterflies in your stomach when you're with her, then that's real love.' Does your mom give you butterflies, Maddy?"

Maddy blinked, taken aback by the question. "What do you mean?"

Chip paused, reflecting on the wisdom of his late aunt. "Yes, every time I'm with her. I have never been sure of anything in my life. I love your mom, Maddy, and I'd love to have your blessing to be with her."

Maddy stared at him for a long moment before her face softened. "Wow, Chip. I did not realize how much you care for her. I am still struggling with the age difference, but I see the love you two have for each other. It is real. You have my blessing. I'll go to the house before the New Year and make things right with Mom."

Chip smiled, relieved. "Thanks, Maddy. And by the way, you might have a baby brother or sister on the way."

Maddy's eyes widened. "I know! I am a little excited "she admitted, a grin creeping onto her face.

"Me too," Chip said, feeling a mix of shock and excitement at the thought of becoming a father.

After their conversation, Chip and Maya headed to the restaurant, where the detectives were finishing their final sweep. Jane had stayed home to rest and recuperate. Maya was taken aback by the state of the restaurant—it had been trashed. Broken dishes, shattered glass, and debris were scattered everywhere. Maya knew Jane could not see it in this condition, especially now that she was pregnant.

Chip and Maya worked side by side, cleaning up the mess. It was a long day, but they slowly began to restore the restaurant. Two hours later, the detectives finished their search and gave them the green light to clean up. "Alright, guys. We have finished here," the lead detective called out.

"Thanks," Chip replied, grateful for permission.

For the next eight hours, Chip and Maya worked tirelessly to get the restaurant back in shape. They rearranged tables, cleaned up the broken glass, and wiped down every surface. By the end of the day, the restaurant was finally ready to reopen in the New Year.

"Hey, how about we grab some burgers before we head home?" Maya suggested, eager for a break.

"Sounds good to me," Chip agreed, grateful for the chance to relax.

Maya took him to a local burger joint called "The Rusty Saw," just a mile down the road. It was a small, unassuming place, but the food was fantastic. After placing their orders—Maya opted for the "Avocado Tornado Burger," and Chip chose the "Bussin Bleu Burger"—they sat down in a quiet corner booth, enjoying the peace.

"I can't believe Mom's pregnant," Maya said, shaking her head in disbelief. "I've always wanted another sibling."

Chip chuckled softly. "Yeah, I'm still processing it too. The shock has worn off, and now I'm just excited to see what's next."

Maya smiled. "It's kind of strange, though, that you're going to be a dad."

"I know, right? I was always the quiet one in high school, keeping to myself. I did not want any drama. I was just trying to figure things out. But now that I've got a plan, I feel a lot more at peace with everything."

"What's your plan, Chip?" Maya asked, intrigued.

Chip's eyes lit up as he spoke. "Well, after I finish my degree in Hotel/Restaurant Management, I want to open my own restaurant, just like your dad did."

"That's amazing!" Maya exclaimed, clearly impressed. "My mom's been such a mentor to you. She is showing you the ropes, right?"

"Exactly. I've learned so much from her."

"Well, when you get established, I'd love to be your Assistant Manager!" Maya grinned. "I've learned a lot from Dad, and I have experience."

Chip smiled. "That sounds like a great idea! But wait, aren't you studying to be a teacher?"

"I am, but I might not do that forever," Maya replied. "I like to keep my options open."

Chip laughed, enjoying the ease of their conversation. "You know, Maya, you're really attractive. Why don't you have a boyfriend?"

Maya paused for a moment, then shrugged. "I'm just not ready for a relationship right now. I want to focus on my studies."

"I get it," Chip said, nodding in understanding. "I was the same way when I first met your mom. I started doing odd jobs around her house, and when I looked into her brown eyes, I fell head over heels in love with her. It was like a powerful connection."

"Was it like butterflies in your stomach?" Maya asked, intrigued.

"Exactly like that," Chip replied. "My aunt actually asked me the same thing before the car accident. She was not thrilled about the age difference, but she said, 'If you feel butterflies when you're with her, that's the person you're meant to be with.'"

"Aww, your aunt sounds so sweet," Maya said, her voice softening.

"She was. Exceptionally beautiful," Chip said with a bittersweet smile.

After finishing their burgers, Chip ordered two milkshakes to go. They chatted a bit longer, and Chip felt a deeper connection with Maya. He appreciated her honesty and the bond they were forming. As they left the diner, Maya felt more at ease with the changes in her family. The future was uncertain, but one thing was clear—they were all in this together.

Chapter 13

Maddy and Jane had a heart-to-heart conversation, resolving the tension from their argument on Christmas. This open and honest discussion allowed them to better understand each other's emotions, leading to a newfound respect for one another's perspectives. As a result, Maddy had fully embraced Chip into her life, and her relationship with Officer Jeff had grown stronger, blossoming into something serious. On New Year's Day, Maddy made a joyous announcement that her and Officer Jeff were engaged to be married. Jane was genuinely thrilled for Maddy and wholeheartedly supported her decision.

In a beautiful moment, Maddy asked Maya to be her maid of honor and requested that her late father's friend, also named Bill, walk her down the aisle. Jane shared her gratitude, expressing how glad she was that Maddy had found someone who absolutely loved her and would cherish her for life. The wedding was set for the fall, just after the arrival of Jane and Chip's baby.

At six months pregnant with a baby boy, Jane's life was filled with excitement. Chip and Jane had been working tirelessly to prepare the spare bedroom for their new son. Maya, thrilled at the idea of having a baby brother, had already begun making plans to spoil him, while Chip could not be happier about becoming a father.

Aware of the importance of planning for the future, Jane had been meeting with her lawyer to update her Last Will and Testament and life insurance policy. With Bill's passing, the girls growing older, and the impending arrival of her baby boy, she felt it was crucial to ensure everything was in place to protect her loved ones in case of the worst.

The decision regarding the baby's name, however, remained unresolved. Jane had suggested naming the baby Chip Eugene Urban Jr., but Chip was adamant about not passing down his name. He wanted their child to have his own identity. After much deliberation, they narrowed down their options to a few names: Jeremy, Jack, David, Brian, and James.

During one of Jane's doctor's appointments, Chip and Maya accompanied her. Maya had become an integral part of their family. After transferring to Montclair Community College to be closer to home and offer support, Maya was excelling in her studies. With only two semesters left before student teaching, she was focused and determined. The bond between the three of them had grown stronger, and they felt like a true family unit.

At the appointment, the doctor performed an ultrasound to check on the baby's development. Everything seemed perfect, the baby's heartbeat was strong, and his feet were clearly visible on the screen. After discussing name options, Jane and Chip finally agreed on the name "James Brian Urban."

"That's a beautiful name for my baby brother!" Maya exclaimed.

"It is a wonderful name," Jane replied, smiling brightly. "It's perfect," Chip added, grinning from ear to ear.

The doctor handed Jane a picture of the sonogram and offered some advice. "Mrs. Davis, you're entering your third trimester. I recommend taking it easy from here on out. This is just a precautionary measure, especially considering you're an older expectant mother."

Jane immediately grew concerned. "Why? Is something wrong with James that you are not telling me?"

"No, no, everything looks great," the doctor reassured her. "This is simply to ensure your safety and the baby's. I recommend minimizing stress and limiting physical activity as much as possible."

"I understand, Doctor," Jane responded, still a bit uneasy.

"Don't worry, honey. We have everything covered," Chip reassured her, gently squeezing her hand. "With Maya's help, I'll take care of the restaurant, and you just focus on you and the baby."

"Of course! Mom, you need to rest and relax with James," Maya added with a supportive smile.

"You two are the best," Jane whispered, touched by their kindness.

The Waiter and Mrs. Davis
By: Keith P. Mulrooney

"Did you hear that, James?" Jane rubbed her stomach lovingly, her face lit up with a joyful smile. "We're going to bond so much over the next three months. I can't wait to tell you all my stories."

Following the doctor's advice, Jane made the decision to take a step back from the Del-Ray restaurant, allowing Chip and Maya to take over the responsibilities. She was ready to focus on herself and her baby for the remainder of her pregnancy, confident that her family would be there for her every step of the way.

Chapter Fourteen

The morning of Jane's labor arrived quietly, the sun barely peeking through the bedroom curtains. Jane had been in labor for several hours, with contractions growing more intense by the minute. Still, she was determined to bring their son, James, into the world. Chip stayed by her side the entire time, his face a mixture of excitement and concern, while Maya was there, too helping in any way she could, offering words of encouragement, and holding Jane's hand through each painful contraction. Over the past months, the three of them had become an inseparable family, and at that moment, they leaned on each other more than ever before.

"I'm so ready to meet him," Jane whispered between breaths, her voice soft but filled with anticipation. "I can't wait to see his little face."

Chip squeezed her hand, offering a reassuring smile. "We're almost there, honey. You're doing great."

But Jane's face tightened with pain, and she gripped the sides of the bed, letting out a sharp gasp. "I don't know how much longer I can take this."

Maya leaned down, her voice gentle in Jane's ear. "You're so strong, Mom. Just a little bit longer. You've got this."

With a final, determined push, Jane gave birth to a beautiful baby boy. His tiny cries filled the room—a sound that should have brought joy yet left Chip and Maya breathless with emotion. Jane, exhausted and weak from the labor, gazed up at Chip with tears in her eyes.

"He's perfect, Chip," she whispered, her voice strained as she looked down at their son. "Our little James."

Chip held their newborn son in his arms, his heart swelling with love. "He's perfect, Jane. You did it. You brought him into this world."

But then, Jane's face grew pale, and her breathing became shallow. Chip's concern deepened as he glanced up at Maya, who was standing near the door, fighting back tears. Before they could react, the room filled with urgency as doctors and nurses rushed in.

"What's happening?!" Chip demanded, panic creeping into his voice as he looked from one medical professional to another.

"She's hemorrhaging," one of the nurses said, her voice frantic. "We need to stabilize her right now."

Despite their best efforts, it quickly became clear that Jane's body could not manage the complications from birth. The doctors worked tirelessly, but her condition continued to worsen. Chip refused to leave her side, gripping her hand tightly and speaking softly to her, trying to keep her conscious.

"Jane, I need you to hold on," he whispered desperately. "Please, don't leave me. Don't leave James."

But Jane, pale and weak, could barely keep her eyes open. "Chip," she whispered, her voice barely audible. "Promise me… you'll take care of him… you'll love him with all your heart."

"Of course, Jane. I will. I promise," Chip cried, his tears flowing freely. "I'll take care of him, and I'll always keep you in my heart."

Jane gave him one last, faint smile before her eyes closed, her hand slipping from his. The monitors beeped once, then flatlined. The room fell into an eerie silence.

"No… no, please!" Chip screamed, his voice raw with pain and disbelief as he clutched her hand. He refused to accept that she was gone. Maya stood frozen at the door, her own heart shattering as she watched Chip crumble.

The nurses quietly left the room, leaving Chip and Maya with Jane's lifeless body and their newborn son, who was still in Chip's arms. Maya rushed to his side, her tears falling freely as she wrapped her arms around him in a tight hug.

"Chip, I'm so sorry," she whispered, her voice thick with sorrow.

But Chip could not speak. His grief consumed him entirely. His heart shattered into a million pieces, each one a cruel reminder of the woman he had lost—the love of his life. His world had come crashing down.

For the next few days, Chip became a shell of the man he had been. He barely ate, hardly slept, and could not bear to look at baby James without being overcome with grief. His son, who was meant to bring joy into their lives, had become a constant reminder of the one person he could never replace. Chip's depression was palpable, and it weighed heavily on Maya, who did her best to support him in every way she could.

Maya became Chip's anchor. She ensured he ate, even when he did not want to. She sat with him in the silence of the house, offering what comfort she could when the weight of it all felt too heavy to bear. She cared for James when Chip could not bring himself to, but she knew she could not fill the void that Jane had left.

One night, Chip sat on the porch, staring blankly into the night sky. Maya joined him, sitting beside him in silence. Their shoulders brushed, but neither of them spoke, both lost in their own thoughts. Finally, Chip broke the silence.

"I can't do this," he said, his voice thick with emotion. "I do not know how to go on without her, Maya. I do not know how to raise James without Jane. She was everything."

Maya reached out, placing a hand on his. "I know, Chip. I know. But you do not have to do it alone. I am here. We are all here for you. And we will get through this. For James. For Jane."

Chip looked at her, his eyes filled with both gratitude and despair. "How do I move forward without her?"

Maya looked down at her lap, taking a deep breath before responding. "You take it one day at a time. You keep her in your heart, and you raise James the way she would have wanted. You do not have to do it all at once. We will take it one step at a time."

Chip's eyes, though red-rimmed and tired, held a glimmer of hope. "I don't know if I can do this without her, but I'll try. For James."

"That's all we can do," Maya said softly, her voice steady. "Just take it one day at a time."

With that, Chip finally allowed his tears to fall. It was the first time he had truly let himself grieve. Maya remained by his side, offering silent comfort in the darkest of moments.

Together, they sat under the stars that had once filled Jane's eyes with dreams of the future. While the pain of her loss would never fully fade, they had each other—and James—to keep her memory alive.

Chapter Fifteen

The first year of James' life passed in a blur of sleepless nights, quiet moments, and overwhelming emotions. Chip had never imagined raising his son alone, especially without Jane by his side. The grief of her loss still loomed over him, an ever-present shadow, but his love for James was his anchor. Each day, as James grew and developed, Chip saw glimpses of Jane in him—the way his eyes sparkled when he laughed, the shape of his tiny hands, the way he would curl up against Chip's chest, seeking comfort. It was painful, but also beautiful. James had become his reason to keep moving forward.

Maya, too, had become an unwavering source of support. She had moved in after Jane's passing, not as a replacement, but as someone who loved both Chip and James in her own way. Though she was still finishing her final semester at Montclair Community College, Maya had devoted herself to being a steady presence in James' life, offering help wherever she could.

Over time, the bond between Maya and James deepened. Maya had always been fond of children, and James was no exception. As a toddler, James adored her. He would smile whenever she walked into a room, his chubby little hands reaching for her, his giggles filling the air. Maya would scoop him up, showering him with kisses, and in those moments, Chip felt a sense of peace, knowing that James had someone who cared for him in such a unique way.

As the months passed, Maya began to see James as more than just Chip's son, she began to see him as family. She spent hours playing with him, reading stories to him, and helping him take his first steps. Maya even started teaching him simple words, pointing at objects, and saying their names, and James would repeat them with a giggle, his voice filled with innocence and wonder.

But it was not just Maya who noticed the bond growing between them. Chip, too, had started relying on Maya in ways he had not expected. The woman who had once been his daughter's best friend had become his ally in this new chapter of his life. Maya had stepped into a maternal role, one that Chip had never asked for but had desperately needed. She had helped him carry a weight he never could have imagined.

The Waiter and Mrs. Davis
By: Keith P. Mulrooney

Chip would often look over the two of them—Maya holding James, rocking him gently to sleep, or playing with him in the living room—and feel a strange mixture of gratitude and sadness. He was thankful for Maya's presence, for how she had stepped in and filled a role that Jane should have been in, but he could not help but mourn Jane's absence. Jane should have been the one raising their son, not Maya.

One evening, as James lay peacefully asleep in his crib, Maya and Chip sat on the porch, the soft hum of crickets filling the silence around them. The night air was cool, and the glow of the porch light cast gentle shadows over their faces.

"Chip," Maya began, her voice quiet, "I can't imagine how hard this has been for you, raising James without Jane."

Chip stared out into the distance, his face a portrait of sorrow. "It has been the hardest thing I have ever done. Every day feels like a battle. But James—he keeps me going. He reminds me of Jane in so many ways. Sometimes, it is hard to look at him and not feel that ache in my chest. But he is also the reason I keep waking up in the morning."

Maya nodded, her eyes soft with understanding. "I know. I see how much you love him. And I see how much he loves you. But Chip, you do not have to do this alone."

Chip looked over at her, his eyes filled with a mixture of exhaustion and gratitude. "I do not know what I would have done without you, Maya. You have been more helpful than I could ever put into words. But I am still struggling. I do not know how to be both a father and a mother to him."

Maya reached over and placed a hand on his. "You do not have to be both. You are his father, and that is enough. And I will be here—always. You are not alone in this."

For a long time, neither of them spoke. The silence between them was heavy, yet somehow comforting. They did not need to say anything more; the weight of their words hung in the air, a mutual understanding of the difficult road ahead. But in that silence, there was solace—a quiet assurance that they had each other.

The year passed much the same way. James hit milestone after milestone: his first steps, his first words, his first birthday. Maya was there for every moment, and Chip found himself relying on her more than ever. When James cried for attention, it was Maya who would scoop him up, comforting him with gentle words and soft lullabies. When Chip needed a break, Maya would step in, taking care of James while Chip found moments of peace in the quiet of the house.

It was not just about survival anymore. They were building a life together—a new family, one born out of necessity but strengthened by love and support. Maya's role in James' life grew even more significant as the months went by. She became a second mother to him, and Chip saw their bond deepen with each passing day.

One afternoon, as they sat in the backyard, James's toddling around the grass while Maya and Chip relaxed under the shade of a tree, Chip found himself smiling in a way he had not seen in a long time.

"Look at him," Chip said softly, his eyes fixed on James, who was attempting to chase after a butterfly. "He is growing so fast. Sometimes, I wish I could freeze time, just so I do not miss anything."

Maya chuckled softly. "I know what you mean. It feels like just yesterday he was a tiny baby, and now he is already walking and getting into everything.

Chip turned to her; his voice was sincere. "Thank you, Maya. For everything. For being here. For being with him. I never could have gotten through this without you."

Maya smiled, her eyes glistening with unshed tears. "I am just doing what Jane would have wanted. Taking care of both of you. You are my family too, Chip. And James—he is my little brother now."

Chip's heart swelled with emotion. He had never expected to be in this position, but looking at Maya and James, he realized they had found a way forward. It was not the life he had imagined, but it was a life he would fight for, every single day. For Jane. For James. And for the family they had become.

Chapter Sixteen

The journey had been long and difficult for Chip and Maya. Over the past few years, they have developed a deep, unspoken bond. Their shared grief, the late-night conversations, and their mutual commitment to raising James together had solidified their relationship in ways neither of them had anticipated. But now, with James growing older, their lives were beginning to change once again.

It was a sunny morning in early fall when Chip and Maya found themselves sitting across from each other at the kitchen table. The soft hum of the coffee maker filled the silence as they sipped their coffee. James had just started preschool, his small backpack slung over his tiny shoulders. They had seen him off that morning, both feeling a mixture of pride and nostalgia. It was a moment they had both anticipated, but it also marked how much James had grown. And as James ventured into this new chapter, Chip and Maya were on the verge of starting one of their own.

Maya took a deep breath, her fingers absentmindedly tapping the edge of her coffee mug. "I can't believe James is already in preschool. It feels like just yesterday he was crawling around the house."

Chip chuckled softly, leaning back in his chair. "I know. Time really does fly. But I am proud of him. He's so ready for this."

Maya smiled, her heart swelling with affection. "He's a smart kid, Chip. He's going to do great things."

A quiet moment passed as they exchanged a look that spoke volumes. It was not just about James anymore; it was about them, too. Over the past year, their connection has deepened in ways neither of them had expected. The grief they both carried was still there, but it was slowly being replaced by something new, something hopeful.

Chip broke the silence, his voice quieter than usual. "Maya, I've been thinking..."

Maya looked up, her brow furrowing slightly in concern. "What's on your mind?"

Chip hesitated, searching for the right words. "I don't know how to say this, but... I am ready for something more. For us, I mean. I have been thinking about it a lot lately, and I feel like I need to say it. I think we've always had this connection, this understanding of each other, and I can't ignore it anymore."

Maya's heart skipped a beat. She had felt the same way, but hearing Chip say it aloud made it even more real. For so long, she had pushed the idea of a relationship with Chip aside, fearing it might complicate things. But now, with James becoming more independent and their lives growing more intertwined, she could not deny the pull she felt toward him.

"I've been thinking the same thing," Maya replied, her voice soft but steady. "I just didn't know if it was the right time. But… maybe it is."

Chip's eyes softened, and he reached across the table to take her hand. "I know it's complicated. I know we've both been through a lot. But I cannot imagine my life without you in it, Maya. You have been by my side through everything, and I" He paused, searching for the right words. "I care about you. More than I ever thought I would."

Maya's chest tightened with emotion. She had never expected to find love amid all the pain, but somehow, it had blossomed between them. "I care about you too, Chip. And I always will. I'm here for you—for both you and James, no matter what."

They shared a quiet, heartfelt moment, the weight of their emotions settling around them. They did not have all the answers, and they were not sure what the future held, but at that moment, they knew they had each other.

As the weeks passed, Chip and Maya's relationship continued to evolve. They spent more time together going on quiet walks in the park, cooking dinner as a family, and sitting on the porch in the evenings, talking about everything and nothing at all. Their connection deepened, and slowly, the grief that had once consumed them began to make room for the possibility of happiness.

James, for his part, had taken to preschool like a fish to water. He loved his new teachers and made friends every day. Chip had been nervous about how James would adjust, but seeing his son excited about going to school each morning filled him with a sense of relief. It was proof that James was growing, learning, and thriving in ways that made Chip proud.

The Waiter and Mrs. Davis
By: Keith P. Mulrooney

One afternoon, after picking James up from school, Chip and Maya sat in the car, watching as James ran toward them with a big grin on his face. His backpack bounced with each step, and his excitement was contagious.

"Guess what, Daddy?" James said breathlessly, his little hands clutching a piece of paper. "I made a picture for you!"

Chip grinned, his heart swelling with pride. "What is it, buddy?"

James handed him the paper, which was covered in bright colors and scribbles that looked like a chaotic masterpiece. "It's a picture of our house! See? That is, you, and that's me, and that's Maya!" he said, pointing to the crayon drawings.

Maya leaned over to get a closer look, her eyes softening. "It's beautiful, James. You did such a wonderful job!"

Chip's throat tightened as he looked at the picture. In that moment, he realized just how much their little family had grown. It was not just him and James anymore. Maya had become a permanent part of their world in a way he had not imagined, and James had accepted her as a constant presence in his life.

"Thank you, buddy," Chip said, his voice thick with emotion. "This is the best picture ever."

As they drove home, James chattered away in the backseat, Maya's hand found Chip's. He squeezed it gently, grateful for her presence, for the love they were slowly allowing to grow between them. It was not easy, and it was not perfect, but it was real. And in that moment, Chip felt more at peace than he had in a long time.

For the first time in years, Chip allowed himself to hope. To believe that despite the pain and the loss, life could still hold beauty, joy, and love. And with Maya by his side, he knew they could build a future together.

Chapter Seventeen

It had started like any other evening. Maya had spent the afternoon with James at the park, watching him run around and play with other children while Chip worked at the restaurant. The warm autumn air wrapped around them, the sound of laughter filling the air as the leaves rustled gently in the breeze. When James tripped while chasing after a ball and scraped his knee, Maya quickly cleaned the wound, offering soothing words and gentle kisses to ease his discomfort. She felt a deep, almost maternal sense of protectiveness over James, as though he were her own child.

By the time they arrived home that evening, something was different. James was not his usual energetic self. He complained of a headache and began to shiver, even though the house was warm. Maya noticed the change immediately, her heart sinking as she kept a close eye on him.

Chip had just returned home from the restaurant, wiping his hands on a towel when he found Maya sitting beside James on the couch, rubbing his forehead.

"Hey, how's he doing?" Chip asked, his voice soft, already filled with concern as he took in the sight of his son looking so vulnerable.

Maya looked up, her face tense with worry. "I think he's coming down with something. He's warm to the touch, and he keeps saying his head hurts."

Chip's stomach was clenched, a knot of anxiety forming in his chest. "Should we take him to the doctor?"

"I think we should wait a little longer," Maya replied, her voice calm but strained. "He's been really active today, and sometimes kids get run down. It's probably just a little bug."

Chip nodded, though the unease in his chest did not go away. He watched as Maya gently tried to soothe James, offering him a glass of water, and tucking him in with his favorite blanket. The evening stretched on like this, with Maya providing comfort while Chip struggled to keep his growing concern in check.

But by midnight, James's condition had worsened. He had developed a fever that would not break. His body was too hot to touch, and he was restless, crying out in discomfort. The fever made him delirious at times, his tiny body trembling under the covers as he struggled to stay awake.

Chip could no longer ignore the panic rising inside him. "Maya, we need to take him to the ER. Right now," he said urgently, his voice sharp with fear.

Maya hesitated, torn between her own concern and the rational side of her mind. "Chip, I think it's just a fever. Kids get them all the time. If we take him to the hospital, he might be exposed to more germs. It could be worse for him."

"Don't you think I know that?" Chip snapped, his temper flaring as his fear intensified. "But what if it's something more serious? What if we are waiting too long?"

Maya stood up, her eyes wide with both concern and frustration. "I'm not saying we shouldn't take him to the doctor, Chip. I am just trying to stay calm. You are panicking, and that is not going to help anyone!"

Chip stepped forward, his voice trembling with emotion. "I'm not panicking! I am trying to protect him, Maya! I cannot lose him. I can't lose another person I love."

Maya flinched at his words, the rawness of his fear hitting her like a physical blow. She had always known about his grief—the pain from losing Jane—but hearing the anguish in his voice made her ache for him in a way she had not expected. She wanted to calm him down, but part of her was angry too, angry at how their differing ways of coping with stress were driving a wedge between them.

"Chip, I know you're scared," Maya said, her voice quieter now but still heavy with emotion. "But you have to trust me. I know what I am doing. I'm not going to let anything happen to James."

Chip turned away, running a hand through his hair in frustration. "I know you care about him, Maya. But it is different for me. I've already lost so much."

"Chip, stop," Maya interrupted, stepping toward him. "I understand. I know how much you're hurting, but I can't do this if you're always second-guessing everything I do."

The words hung heavily between them. For a long moment, neither of them spoke, the tension thick with unspoken emotions. Their conflicting fears were starting to tear at them during a crisis they couldn't control.

It was James who broke the silence, his weak voice cutting through the air. "Daddy? I don't feel good."

Maya's heart broke at the sight of him. His tiny face, flushed with fever, twisted with discomfort. Without thinking, she rushed to his side, brushing his damp hair away from his forehead. "I'm right here, sweetheart," she whispered, her voice steady as she tried to comfort him, despite the panic rising inside her.

Chip stood frozen for a moment, his anger slipping away, replaced by helplessness. Seeing James in pain hit him harder than anything else. His protective instinct surged to the forefront. He stepped forward, placing a hand on James's small shoulder. His voice was thick with emotion. "We're going to make sure you're okay, buddy. No matter what. We're here."

Maya met his gaze, her eyes softening as she took in the sincerity of his words. "Chip, we'll do whatever it takes to help him. Let's get him checked out."

Chip nodded; his breath shaky as he exhaled a sigh, he had not realized he was holding. Together, they bundled James up and rushed him to the hospital, the drive filled with a strained silence. Neither of them wanted to admit how close they had come to breaking apart over something that felt so minor compared to what was really at stake—James's health.

At the hospital, they were quickly ushered into a private room. After a battery of tests, the doctor finally confirmed what Maya had suspected all along: It was just a viral fever, caused by a simple cold or flu. James would be okay, but they needed to monitor him closely for the next few days to make sure the fever broke.

Exhausted and emotionally drained, Chip and Maya sat beside James in the hospital room. The quiet beeping of the machines monitoring his vital signs filled the otherwise still air. Maya held James in her lap, gently rocking him back and forth, while Chip leaned against the wall, eyes closed, trying to regain his composure.

"I'm sorry," Chip muttered after a long silence, his voice barely above a whisper. "I shouldn't have yelled at you earlier. I was scared, and I took it out on you."

Maya looked up at him, her expression softening. "I know. I was scared too. But we cannot let fear tear apart, Chip. We are in this together, okay? You don't have to go through this alone."

He nodded, swallowing hard, then walked over to her. Taking a seat beside her, he looked down at James, still sleeping peacefully in her arms. "I don't know what I would do without you, Maya. I know I have been distant, but... I cannot lose him. I can't lose anyone else."

Maya squeezed his hand, offering him a small but meaningful smile. "You won't lose us, Chip. We are your family. We're all in this together."

For the first time that night, Chip felt a weight lift off his chest. He still had his fears, his doubts, but at that moment, as he looked at Maya and James, he knew that no matter what, they were stronger together.

Chapter Eighteen

The night had dragged on, filled with worry and exhaustion, but now, as the soft hospital lights dimmed and the chaos of the day began to fade into a quiet calm, a sense of peace settled over the room. James was finally asleep, his fever broken, his tiny body finally resting after hours of discomfort. Chip and Maya sat in the stillness of the hospital room, the world outside continuing its course, but for them, time had slowed.

Maya sat by the window, her back to Chip, gazing out at the city lights twinkling far off in the distance. The glow of the lights seemed to symbolize a quiet promise—a reminder that life, though unpredictable, always found a way to keep going. Chip, exhausted but relieved, stood by the door, his eyes following Maya's figure. She had always been a steady presence for him, especially during the hardest moments of his life. Tonight, with James on the mend, he felt an overwhelming sense of gratitude and love for her. Maya had been his rock, and in this stillness, with the future uncertain but their love unwavering, he knew with every fiber of his being that he could not let her go.

"Maya," Chip's voice broke the silence, soft but firm, drawing her attention.

She turned slowly, a tired but genuine smile on her face. "Chip, I'm just so happy he's going to be okay." Her voice trailed off, a look of quiet relief in her eyes. There were no more words needed—her emotions were there for anyone to see.

Chip nodded, stepping closer. "Me too. But I have been thinking…" He paused for a moment, his eyes never leaving her face. "I can't imagine going through all of this without you. I never thought I would get to this place, but I feel like we have built something real. Something worth fighting for."

Maya's heart ached with emotion; the weight of his words settled deep within her. She had always known their bond was something special but hearing him say it aloud made her feel it more deeply. "I feel the same way, Chip. You and James have become my world. I've never loved anyone the way I love both of you."

Chip moved closer still, his hand reaching out to gently take hers. The touch was soft, yet there was a quiet intensity in his eyes. It was not just gratitude; it was a deeper, undeniable feeling that had been growing for months—years, even—and tonight, it could no longer be contained.

"I want to ask you something, Maya." His voice was barely above a whisper, carrying a weight of emotion.

Maya's heart skipped a beat, a surge of anticipation flooding her chest. She had no idea what was coming, but she could sense the gravity of the moment. "What is it?"

Chip took a deep breath, gathering the courage to finally say what he had been holding onto for so long. "I know we have been through a lot, and it's not the right time, but I can't wait any longer. I love you, Maya. I love you with everything I have. And I want to build a life with you. I want to be your partner… forever."

Maya blinked, her breath catching in her throat. She had been waiting for this moment, hoping for it, in one way or another—but hearing him say it so openly, so vulnerable, made her heart swell. She felt as though her entire world had shifted in that single instant.

Chip reached into his pocket, his movements slow and deliberate. He pulled out a small velvet box and opened it, revealing a simple but beautiful ring—perfect for Maya, perfect for the life they had built together. He looked into her eyes, his own filled with hope and love.

"Maya," he said, his voice thick with emotion, "will you marry me? Will you make me the happiest man alive and be my wife?"

Tears filled Maya's eyes as she looked from the ring to Chip, overwhelmed by the rawness of the moment. This was everything she had dreamed of everything she had hoped for, and yet somehow, it felt even more real than she could have imagined. In that moment, everything they had been through—every loss, every struggle—had led her here, to this place, with Chip and James. They were her family now.

"Yes," she whispered, her voice shaking with emotion. "Yes, I will marry you, Chip. I love you."

Chip exhaled a relieved laugh, his eyes lighting up with joy as he slid the ring onto her finger. He pulled her into his arms, holding her close, as if he never wanted to let go. The weight of everything they had endured, the tough times, the doubts, the pain—seemed to dissolve in that moment, leaving only the love they had fought so hard to nurture.

Maya kissed him gently, her heart full, as Chip wrapped his arms around her tightly. It was not just about the ring or the proposal; it was about everything they had built together, the shared moments, the quiet strength they had given each other through the hardest of times. The love they shared was not perfect, but it was real, and at that moment, it felt like the only thing that truly mattered.

They stood there, holding each other in the quiet of the hospital room, the world outside continuing, while they made their quiet promise to one another. This was the beginning of something new, something stronger than either of them could have ever imagined.

After a long moment, Chip spoke again, his voice tender, almost reverent. "I am so glad you said yes, Maya. I do not know what the future holds, but with you by my side, I feel like we can face anything."

Maya smiled, resting her head against his chest. "We will face it together, Chip. No matter what."

As they stood there, wrapped in each other's arms, the world outside seemed to pause for just a moment. In that brief, suspended second, they were no longer two individuals simply trying to make it through the tough times. They were partners now, with a shared future ahead of them. A future that, despite the hardships they had already faced, was filled with hope, love, and the promise of new beginnings.

For the first time in a long while, Chip felt a weight lift from his shoulders. And as he kissed Maya softly, he knew, deep in his heart, that their love had finally come full circle, stronger than it had ever been before.

Chapter Nineteen

The weeks following Chip's proposal were a whirlwind of excitement and anticipation. Maya and Chip, alongside a close-knit group of family and friends, dove headfirst into the planning of their wedding. The ceremony would be held at Del-Ray Restaurant and Banquet Hall, the very place where Chip had rebuilt his life after so much loss. For Chip, the restaurant was more than just a business he took over after Jane's passing; it was a symbol of second chances of new beginnings, and the foundation on which their love had grown.

Maya, with her impeccable organizational skills and her love for detail, took the reins of most of the planning. Chip, although not the most organized person, was fully involved, ensuring every aspect of the day was exactly right. Together, they made the perfect team, each complementing the other in ways that made them stronger.

The ceremony was scheduled for a crisp, clear autumn afternoon, only a few days after James' fourth birthday. It would be an intimate gathering, with just their closest friends and family. The restaurant had been transformed into a stunning wedding venue, adorned with soft white lights and elegant fall-themed decorations—rich golds, deep reds, and vibrant oranges—creating a warm, inviting atmosphere that felt both personal and magical.

Maya had chosen a simple yet breathtaking gown—an ivory dress with delicate lace accents, the hem just long enough to sweep the floor as she walked. Her beauty radiated in the soft light, her smile the highlight of her entire look. Chip, ever understated, wore a sharp navy-blue suit, his deep burgundy tie matching the wedding theme. As Maya prepared to walk down the aisle, Chip looked at her with a kind of love that made his heart swell with pride.

James, their playful and curious little boy, had been given the special role of ring bearer. He wore a miniature tuxedo to match Chip is, his tiny hands gripping the pillow that carried the rings. It was too big for him, but he was determined to perform his duty with seriousness. As he walked down the aisle, he looked at the grown-up, and both Maya and Chip could not help but smile at how much he had grown. James was thrilled to be a part of the ceremony and be included in this significant moment.

The Waiter and Mrs. Davis
By: Keith P. Mulrooney

On the day of the wedding, the sun shone brightly, casting a golden glow over the city. The soft sounds of a string quartet began to fill the air, signaling that it was time for the ceremony to begin. As the guests took their seats, Maya stood in front of the mirror in the back room of the restaurant, her heart racing with excitement. She glanced at Chip, who stood just outside the door, his back to her as he took a deep breath, clearly nervous.

"I'm ready, Maya," he said quietly, his voice shaky with emotion. "I just... I do not want to mess this up."

Maya smiled and walked toward him, her hand gently resting on his arm. "Chip, there is no way you could mess this up. We are already perfect together. Today is about us, our love, and our family. We have made it through so much already. This is just the beginning."

She placed a soft kiss on his cheek, offering him a moment of reassurance. Together, they stepped out from the back room and walked toward the front of the restaurant, where their guests waited with eager anticipation.

As the familiar melody of "Here Comes the Bride" began to play, the doors of the restaurant swung open, revealing Maya in her wedding dress. The room fell silent for a moment, every guest turning to witness the breathtaking bride. Chip's breath caught in his chest as he saw her walking toward him, glowing with happiness. In that instant, the world seemed to stand still—he was seeing her for the first time in this way, and it took his breath away.

Behind her, little James appeared, clutching the pillow with the wedding rings, his small face full of concentration as he carefully made his way down the aisle. The sight of him, trying so hard to take his job seriously, was a moment of pure joy for everyone in the room. Guests smiled and whispered to one another, charmed by how adorable James looked as he proudly took on his responsibility.

When James reached the altar, he handed the pillow to Chip, who gently accepted it, his hands trembling slightly from the weight of the moment. Chip smiled down at his son, offering him a soft pat on the head. "You did great, buddy."

The Waiter and Mrs. Davis
By: Keith P. Mulrooney

Maya stood beside him, looking up at Chip with tears in her eyes. "Are you ready?" she whispered.

Chip smiled, his heart swelling. "I've never been more ready for anything in my life."

The officiant, a longtime friend of the family, began the ceremony, speaking of love, commitment, and family. The spoke of the bond that Chip and Maya had built over the years—a love that had been evaluated through hardship and had only grown stronger. He talked about the promise they were about to make to support, cherish, and love one another for the rest of their lives.

When it was time to exchange vows, Chip and Maya's eyes locked, and the weight of their shared history filled the space between them. They had overcome so much to be here, and now, they were ready to take this step together.

"I, Chip, take you, Maya," Chip said, his voice thick with emotion. "To be my wife, to love and support you through every season of life, for better or for worse. I promise to be here, every day, for you and for James."

Maya, her voice, steady yet soft, spoke next. "I, Maya, take you, Chip, to be my husband. I promise to stand by you, through every joy and every challenge. To love you with all my heart, and to love the beautiful family we have created together."

The officiant smiled warmly, then pronounced the final words: "By the power vested in me, I now pronounce you husband and wife. You may kiss the bride."

With a smile that was both tender and triumphant, Chip leaned in and kissed Maya. The room erupted in applause, their guests cheering and clapping as the couple turned to face them, beaming with happiness and love.

James, excited and proud, clapped his hands vigorously, his face glowing with joy. He had played a part in making this day even more special, and he could not have been more thrilled.

As they walked back down the aisle, hand in hand, James trailing happily behind them, Maya leaned into Chip, her heart full of warmth. "This is just the beginning, isn't it?"

Chip smiled down at her, his arm around her waist. "Yes, it is. The best is yet to come."

Together, they left the altar behind and stepped into their future, a family bound by love and the promise of new beginnings. This day would forever be etched in their hearts as the moment they started their new life together.

Chapter Twenty

The sun hung low in the sky, casting a warm golden hue over the sleepy streets of their neighborhood. Chip and Maya walked side by side, their hands brushing occasionally as they led James down the sidewalk toward his new adventure. Today was the first day of kindergarten, a milestone that seemed to come so quickly, and their little boy was filled with a mix of excitement and nerves. He clutched his new backpack with the kind of pride only a child could muster, his steps quick and eager, yet his eyes flickered with uncertainty.

As they passed the familiar Del-Ray, the place where they had celebrated birthdays, anniversaries, and countless memories, Maya's eyes caught the small, welcoming sign in the window. The restaurant, a symbol of their past, seemed to beckon with its quiet presence. A gentle smile curled on her lips, but her gaze lingered longer than usual, a flutter in her chest reminding her of the secret she had not yet shared with Chip. The weight of the moment grew heavier with each step, but Maya remained silent, her heart full of both anticipation and uncertainty.

"Mom, do you think I'll like kindergarten?" James asked, looking up at her with wide eyes filled with a trace of worry.

Maya crouched down beside him, brushing a stray lock of hair from his forehead, her touch tender and reassuring. "You are going to have a wonderful time, James. You will make lots of new friends, and you will learn so many things that will make you proud of yourself."

Chip smiled, squeezing Maya's hand gently as he looked at their son. "You are going to do amazing, kiddo. I just know it."

The school gates came into view, and Chip knelt beside James, adjusting the straps on his backpack. Maya stood by her heart swelling with a mixture of love and pride. Her little boy was growing up right before her eyes, and it was a beautiful, bittersweet realization. The future was unfolding in ways she never imagined.

Before they said their final goodbyes, Maya felt that familiar flutter again—something deep within her that had been growing for weeks, a change on the horizon that she could no longer keep to herself. She took a deep breath, her heart pounding in her chest as the moment felt bigger than anything that had come before it.

"Chip," she began, her voice trembling just slightly, "there's something I need to tell you."

Chip paused, looking up at her, his brow furrowing with concern. "What is it?"

Maya hesitated, the words feeling heavier than she had anticipated. She glanced at James, who was bouncing on his heels, his excitement palpable as he eyed the school building, eager to start his first day. Maya smiled at him, then turned back to Chip, her eyes searching for him.

"I'm pregnant," she said softly, the words hanging in the air between them.

For a moment, Chip froze. His hands hovered mid-air, the bustling world around them seemed to fade, the sounds of birds chirping and the chatter of children going unnoticed. Time seemed to stretch for a heartbeat, and in that brief silence, Maya saw the shock in Chip's eyes slowly shift into something else. His expression softened, his lips curling into a smile that made Maya's heart swell.

"Really?" he asked, his voice filled with awe and joy.

Maya nodded, her eyes brimming with tears of happiness. "Yeah. It is going to be another substantial change for us, but I think we're ready for it."

In an instant, Chip stood up, wrapping his arms around her tightly, pulling her close as if they were the only two people in the world. Maya felt a wave of warmth and love flood over her, but before she could fully absorb the moment, James tugged on his father's shirt, oblivious to the weight of the news.

"Dad! Can I go in now?" James's voice was full of excitement and impatience, eager to begin his adventure.

Chip pulled away, giving Maya one last lingering look before turning to his son. "Yeah, friend. Go on in. We will be right here waiting for you when you are done."

James ran ahead, his laughter echoing behind him as he disappeared into the school building. Maya and Chip stood there for a moment, hand in hand, watching the door close behind him. Their son was off to start his journey, and with it, a new chapter of their own lives was unfolding.

The future stretched before them, an unknown path filled with both the comfort of old memories and the excitement of new possibilities. Maya leaned against Chip's shoulder, a quiet smile on her face as she whispered, "I'm so glad we're doing this together."

"Me too," Chip replied, his voice thick with love. "We have this, Maya. All of it."

As the first day of kindergarten began and the world seemed to shift into new rhythms, Maya could not help but feel the quiet promise of a new beginning. It was a new adventure, one she was ready to take on with Chip by her side, and soon, with their growing family. Their journey together was far from over; in fact, it was just beginning.

The Waiter and Mrs. Davis
By: Keith P. Mulrooney

Epilogue

Years had passed since that pivotal autumn day at Del-Ray, and life had changed in ways that Chip and Maya had once only dreamed about. Their family had grown. James, now a bright and curious boy, had a baby sister to dote on. The little one, Lily, filled their home with laughter, and her first giggles were a sound Chip and Maya had come to cherish.

They often found themselves sitting together at the same table at Del-Ray, a place that had been the cornerstone of their story. The restaurant, once a symbol of Chip's painful past, had transformed into a symbol of resilience and love. It had become more than just a place of business, it was a place of memories, of beginnings, and of shared moments that had changed their lives forever. Bill and Jane's legacy was alive in the very walls, the food, and the warmth they had all helped create.

As they watched James's play with his sister in the corner booth, Chip turned to Maya. "You know, sometimes I still can't believe how far we've come."

Maya smiled; her eyes soft with love. "I do. Every day. I think of how hard it was at the beginning and now look at us. We are not just surviving—we are thriving, Chip."

Chip nodded, his gaze lingering on the photo of Bill and Jane that hung proudly on the wall. It had become a tribute, not just to their friendship, but to the deep bond that had grown out of their shared experiences. Chip had never viewed Bill as a mentor, but in the years since his passing, he had come to see how much the restaurant—and Bill and Jane's faith in him—had shaped who he had become. They had given him a second chance, and for that, Chip would always be grateful.

The restaurant buzzed around them with laughter and chatter, the familiar sound of clinking glasses and plates filling the air. Maya reached for Chip's hand, squeezing it gently. "We've built something beautiful, haven't we?"

"We have," Chip replied. "And it's only just beginning."

Their love had been evaluated, but with each challenge, it had only grown stronger. Now, with their children by their side and the future ahead, Chip and Maya knew that no matter what life threw their way, they would face it together.

Family, love, and the promise of tomorrow—this was their life, and they were ready for all the new beginnings it would bring.

The sun set outside, casting a golden glow over the street, and as they shared a quiet moment together, Chip knew that the past had brought them here. And from this place, everything was possible.